ZACHERY

THE PRIDE OF THE DOUBLE DEUCE BOOK 6

KATHI S. BARTON

This is a work of fiction. Names, characters, places, and incidents are products of the author's imagination or are used fictitiously and are not to be construed as real. Any resemblance to actual events, locations, organizations, or persons, living or dead, is entirely coincidental.

World Castle Publishing, LLC

Pensacola, Florida

Copyright © Kathi S. Barton 2017

Paperback ISBN: 9781629897097

eBook ISBN: 9781629897103

First Edition World Castle Publishing, LLC, June 29, 2017

http://www.worldcastlepublishing.com

Licensing Notes

Cover: Karen Fuller

Editor: Maxine Bringenberg

ZACHERY

CHAPTER 1

The building and surrounding area looked like a crater. The swing set, which may have held eight on it, was a twisted mess that hung from one of the blackened trees about a mile away. The slide was still sitting in its original place, yet barely resembled its former self. The only reason Harlan knew what it was is because he'd seen his own kids on it. He looked over when someone said his name.

"Four dead. We think. It's going to be a little while before we can sort this mess out. If there were cars in the lot, I'm not sure how long it will take before we can figure out not just the owners, but if they might have been here last night. Christ, this is a mess." Harlan asked him if they'd been able to get a list of teachers yet. "We're still working on that. I have been able to canvas the damage surrounding this land. There has been one death that is apparently related to this explosion, but we won't know for sure until all reports are in. Had this been in the city, Harlan, you know this would have been a hell of a lot worse."

"Yes. There are reports of windows blasted out eight miles from here. And I heard that one of the deaths was a man who had been on the street in front at the impact time and was killed by the blast. Is that the one that you're talking about?" Richard nodded. "As you know, had this happened only about ten hours later, there would have been children here, and a lot more bodies."

"We have narrowed down the center, we're pretty sure. The city planner brought by the blueprints like you asked for, and he's looking things over and thinks he knows where the epicenter is. Second grade room, as near we can tell." Harlan wasn't able to go to the area just yet; the fire department was going over some of the wreckage to make sure that the fires were out. The bomb squad had left about half an hour ago. "The three bodies that we've recovered here so far are two men from the janitorial service and a woman. No ID yet on the latter. We think it might have been the principal, but we're not sure where the person was at when the bomb went off, in or out of the building. But again, we're working on that too."

"Next of kin been notified on the others?" Richard told him not as yet, they were waiting on the cleaning service to get back to them on how many people were here. "Let me know."

When Richard excused himself just as his phone rang, Harlan moved as close to the site as he could get. Whoever had done this, and he had little doubt that a single sick individual was responsible, they'd wanted a high kill rate. And this wasn't a gas explosion like the police were hoping either. A bomb, a huge one, had gone off here.

Eight hours after he had arrived, they found what they thought was the kill switch, and that other bombs had been set up around the building. According to the experts, there was one central location that once detonated, would fire off the other twelve smaller but no less powerful bombs around the large structure. Harlan was also informed that the person who had set this up was good, maybe even an expert. Or they had an understanding of internet jargon better than most.

"Whoever this person was, they wanted this building gone, and didn't care who was inside of it. It had a switch on location, meaning that it was set off by a simple movement or a lid being removed, so it mattered little to them when this thing went off. I would say that it more than likely was triggered by opening whatever it came here in, which I'm thinking cardboard at this point. The others all depended on the main larger bomb, causing enough power to set them off as well. They were on a tumbler-like set off. Once they were moved, hard, they would blow." Harlan asked him how long something like this would take to set up. "Hours. Maybe a few days. The person would have had to have access to the building, and no one to question what they were doing here. A good sense of the size, layout, as well as how much explosive material to use to get this sort of devastation."

"So whoever it was, they were known to those that work here, you're thinking. I mean, the staff here, they didn't have any issues with this person being in and out of here, so they could have pretty much done this without anyone having any clue." Richard nodded. "This is some sick shit, you know that, right? In another few hours, there would have been over four hundred people in this building, mostly kids. And then nearly seventy teachers and other staff."

"Don't forget buses of kids that were being held to drop off at the higher grades, parents here dropping off little Jimmy for his first day, and any of the other hundreds of people that might have been passing by when this went off." Harlan moved through the debris and other mangled things while they talked. "I heard that you're having trouble locating two of the teachers. You think they might have been here too?"

"I hope to Christ not. Also, we did hear from the cleaning service. There were not three here, but six, to get the building ready for the first day. So far we've had no luck at all trying to figure out if they showed up for work or not. The teachers have all been accounted for, except the two you know about. One of them is the one that had that classroom. Tisha Porter." Richard asked him if it was old man Randall's daughter. "I have no idea. Randall Porter a name I should know?"

"Yes. Well, sort of. He's been putting his name around town for a few years now. Probably because his little girl teaches here. If this is her, I can have someone check on it. If it's her that's missing, he'll have a better chance of finding her than you will." Harlan asked him why. "Because he has a supposed endless supply of money, and she's his only child."

At about nine that night, nearly twenty-four hours after the explosion happened, Harlan found himself in Tisha's neighborhood, which made him feel like he was underdressed. Tisha hadn't contacted her father since last evening, nor was she answering her phone. Harlan just knew that he was going to find out that she'd done this and skipped town. According to friends, she was a nice girl and didn't bother others, and that was what gave him the feeling that she was in this deeper than anyone. Harlan hated to have to tell her daddy if he was right. That man was very forceful and concerned at the same time.

There was no car in the drive but he could see one in the garage. The lower level of the building was as big as his entire house. Going to the door, he drew his gun when he saw that the glass nearest the handle had been broken inward. Calling in backup, he was told to wait. It was then that he saw the blood.

"I can't wait. I can see that someone is hurt. Going in."

Instead of letting the dispatcher tell him to wait again, he muted his phone. He could be fired for it if this turned out to be nothing, but right now, he just didn't care.

As he made his way into the house, he noted in an abstract sort of way that it was neat. Not in a cleaned up sort of way — though it was that too — but more like this person did not care for clutter or fluff.

Straight lines and hard surfaces were on everything, including the cushions on the chairs in the kitchen. It was also expensive, like this person spent all their money on their things, as they had no children or pets to muss it. Making his way to the living room, he could see the difference immediately. This was a room that was used; comfort nearly screamed at him.

The noise to his left gave him pause. He wasn't in a good place in the house…the hallway he was in was not only open at both ends with rooms coming out from each side, but there were two doors that were opened in front of him, one on the right, the other on the left. But when he heard it again, he moved forward.

"This is the Nevada Police. I'm armed and have backup." He heard the sirens getting closer and peeked quickly into the room to his right. Nothing. "Ms. Porter? Can you hear me?"

"Yes." He thought he heard her answer him but wasn't sure. "I'm dying. I'm alone." Relief was short lived when she cried out. "She hurt me."

Entering the room at the end, the doorway that spilled into the hall, he nearly backed away. The woman lying in a pool of blood looked as if she was indeed dying. Her body was not only covered in a great many of what looked like knife wounds, but she was beaten up as well. Moving closer, keeping his gun out, Harlan called for an ambulance.

"I'm Harlan James. Are you Tisha Porter?" She nodded, then passed out. He could see that she'd been making notes, and it sickened him that she'd been forced to do this. The papers to her left were covered in bloodied letters that not only spelled out who had hurt her, but also who to call when they found her. Taking her pulse, Harlan thought she was dead for a few seconds until he felt her very faint heartbeat. Then she looked at him again. "Ms. Porter? Can you tell me when this happened?"

"Late. I thought it was the neighbor's cat at the door." He nodded, taking out his phone and setting it to record. "Before I could.... The door, it exploded inward. I was hurt then. Knife. My knife. She used it. Hammer too."

"Can you tell me who?" Before she could say anything, she was out again. And as much as he wanted to shake her awake to answer him, he knew that any movement might well kill her. Harlan looked at the papers.

The name of the other missing teacher was what she had written down as who harmed her. There was a timeline too. At eleven forty-five, the sound at the door. Eleven forty-nine, Alexandra Grace rushed her. Eleven fifty, Alex hit her first with a hammer, then knives. It also said that she'd beaten her. The times were messed up then, the spelling off, but he read this woman's account like she'd been writing up a police report. At six-thirty this morning, Alex had left. The facts in-between those times, he knew, would haunt him for years to come.

By the time the ambulance arrived, he'd called in a report on what he'd found. Then he told his boss what she'd written down about the other teacher, as well as having someone sent to her house to find the woman. Alexandra Grace was going to have a lot of explaining to do.

~~~

Randall moved through the hospital trying to figure out where he was to go. The nurse at the front desk had told him twice how to get to the operating area, but he was hurting in his heart so badly he only half remembered. When he saw two police officers, he made his way to them.

"I'm looking for my daughter, Tisha Porter." The officer nodded at him and then took him to a man dressed in a dark suit. "My daughter, someone said that she was hurt. Tisha Porter is her name. She's a teacher. Second grade. They all just love her."

"I'm Harlan James, Mr. Porter. I came in with her." Randall felt his knees simply give out on him. If Harlan hadn't been there to catch him, he was sure he would have fallen. "Come on over here, Mr. Porter. We'll talk while we wait."

"She loves teaching those children. I saw in the news that the entire building was blown up. I never got much from the man who called me." Harlan said it had been him. "Was she in the building?"

"No. We found her at her home. That's where we're thinking she was hurt. Someone broke in." Randall tried to think of why someone would harm his little girl. "She was beaten, and cut up pretty badly. The doctors here are doing all that they can to save her. You have a very smart and brave daughter, Mr. Porter. She's helped us a great deal in this."

"That's my baby. Always knew she was the best. I spoke to her just last night...I think it was the night before. It's hard to think so much time has.... I had just called her to tell her to have fun with her first day. I teased her about her room being...." He paused, trying to remember something about a box. "She had this mysterious box, she said. Even asked me if I'd sent it to her. I didn't of course, but I told her it was more than likely from one of the other teachers. Perhaps they'd left it there." He asked him the same thing as he had his daughter. "No, no name she told me. Only hers on a Post-It note on the top. I never thought to ask her about the handwriting. I mean, it was just a box, right?"

"The blast came from the general area of where her room would have been. We only know things as they get found. But it is speculated that it was a cardboard box, and like I said, in the area where her room might have been." Randall wanted to ask if they thought his baby had done it. Or if she had been the target of this monstrosity. The officer seemed to understand. "She had left notes on what she knew and what had happened to her. They were with her when I found her in her home. Tisha, she made sure we had enough information to get started on trying to find this.... We're currently looking for someone that might have a connection to what has happened to your daughter. But as of now, we don't believe Tisha had a thing to do with this. We'll know more as our investigation continues."

"She's all I have in the world. Since her mother died, Tisha has become my whole world. I just saw her last weekend, and she was telling me how she'd gotten all these nice learning tools from a shop online. And now this." Harlan told him they were doing their best. "If you need anything, a kick in the ass to the mayor, you let me know. I'll pull some strings and get you more manpower if you need it. You just let me know. I'll get it for you."

"I think we have it for now, but I'll keep that in mind. We're working round the clock now, so I hope to have answers in a few days, if not sooner." Randall nodded and Harlan stood up. "I'm going to have someone at her room until we find this other person. And if you'd be so kind, I'd like for you to have a guard as well. Right now we don't know the reason that any of this happened. So to be on the safe side, I'd like to protect you as well."

"I have my own bodyguards." Randall nodded to the hall where they were and the three men standing there. "Nothing will get past these men unless I tell them or they're dead. If it will free up some of your men, I can assign them to her room as well. To be honest, sir, they'll be there anyway. If you'll agree to it, then nobody will get their underwear all tightened up by them being there too."

"I'll let you know."

Randall nodded then was left alone. Making his way down the hall, he told Burt, his right hand man, what was going on as he sat in one of the most uncomfortable chairs he'd ever been in. He also told Burt to set up some people on the inside for her safety.

"You have it, sir. And may I suggest that we bring in that buddy of yours? The retired agent? He could be a little more help even from the sidelines." Randall nodded. "Very good, sir. Have they told you how she's doing? I mean, more than you were told on the phone?"

"No. I'd very much like it if you can run a check on any doctors and nurses she has contact with. And there is a person of interest that the police are looking for. Another teacher. Find out who this person is and anything you can find about them." Burt said he would put his best on it. "One more thing, I want you to find out about her home. That cop said someone broke into it. Maybe they don't know about the cameras in the house."

"More than likely not. I'll take one of them there with me to check." Randall told him to take Harlan James and to give anything they found to him. He'd know what to do with it.

"Very good. Anything else?"

"I don't think so right now, but I might. He wants a guard put on her room and me. You'll see that things are taken care of here for her. We won't take over, but there isn't any way that I'm leaving this to chance. Someone hurt my little girl." Burt looked pained, and said that he would. Tisha was loved by all that knew her. "We'll help them when we can, Burt, but I won't sit idly by."

"No, sir. That's not your style. Nor that of your daughter. We'll help them, or if nothing is moving we'll get them going." Randall leaned back in the chair, trying to find a position that didn't hurt. At least too much. "Sir, I'm going to find you a hotel, someone to bring you something to eat, as well as a doctor here that knows your condition."

After telling Burt to do what he needed, Randall closed his eyes. He was exhausted, and that didn't play well with his heart. Breathing in and out slowly, like he'd been taught to help himself, he tried to calm his nerves and heart. All he could think about was his daughter.

Tisha had been born later in his life, he'd been nearing forty and his wife just shy of that. Had anyone asked, he would have said they were happy being childless. They had money, a great deal of it, and traveled, and pretty much did anything that they wanted. Then Rachel had gotten pregnant and Tisha had come along. Randall was pretty sure until that moment he'd not lived at all. Hadn't taken a good breath of air, nor had his heart beat so well until he looked into the most beautiful pair of blue eyes he'd ever seen. His baby girl, Tisha Randall Porter.

She'd been the best baby, and an even better child. No temper tantrums were ever thrown, nor did she give them a hard time about things. Of course, he'd made sure that she had everything that she wanted…even if she only gave something a passing glance, he'd get it for her. Until the day she turned seven.

"I want to get a job." He only nodded at her, indulging her even though he knew she'd never have to work a day in her life, if he could help it. "My friend, Emma, has a job. And her grandma pays her for doing the dishes too. Not the pots and pans, but her pretty dishes she serves tea on."

"Tisha, I can give you money if that's what you want. I have no problem with it." She told him no, she wanted to earn her keep. "Honey, you don't have to earn anything. We're very wealthy."

"So are Emma's mommy and daddy. And she has her own pocket money that she can do whatever she wants with and not have to ask. Why last month, she took me to get an ice cream soda, and no one knew about it but just the two of us." Randall wondered just how much this other little girl was teaching his daughter. "I want to do this, Dad. You want me to be smart like you? And know the value of money?"

"I do. And I'm pretty sure that you have a good handle on the value of money." Then she gave him that look. It wasn't a pouty one, like most little girls did, but the kind that told him he was being too much of a dad. He also knew that he'd give her the world should she want it. "All right, child, whatever you want. But I'd like you to keep an accounting of your money and your spending. If you're going to earn your own money, then you're going to be accountable for it as well. Then at the end of one month, we'll see how you did."

He'd thought that after a few weeks she'd tire of what he'd viewed as games. But at the end of a month, she'd come to him with not only her books, as she called them, but receipts on everything she'd spent too. Which wasn't much.

"I've been taking out the trash in the kitchen, and Molly pays me one dollar for doing it. She said that her husband could do it, but he's too busy in the house so I could." Randall had made a mental note to pay back his cook and thank her for what she'd done. "And the gardener gave me five dollars for helping him pick up the twigs in the yard after the storm last week. He said that my back was younger and I was closer to the ground, and that I saved him some pain. I think he needs to have more help, Dad. The man's list is never finished."

Another note to his list of things she'd found out for him. As they went over her books, he was astonished not only at much she had learned by talking to the staff, but how much she'd managed to save up as well. One hundred dollars just by doing odd jobs for those that worked for them.

"All right, let's see how you spent your cash, shall we?" Randall had already had it in his head to get her a real ledger, as well as some colored pencils. It was the way that he'd been keeping track of his earnings for years. Not only did he love seeing the numbers all lined up in neat rows, but when he had gotten a computer and it did the adding for him, he still found himself using his old tried and true method.

"I've put a computer on layaway. I had to have Molly help me with that. They'd not sell me one at my age. I think it's ridiculous that there has to be an age limit on learning, but now that it's there, I pay on it every week and she takes it to the store for me." Randall told her he'd purchase it for her. "No, Dad. I'm doing this on my own."

After an hour of going over everything, he'd needed to find a quiet place to think. She had not just opened his eyes to his staff, but to the fact that she was not a baby any more. Randall would only admit this to himself, but he'd had a good cry over that fact, and still got teary when he thought of it.

16

"Mr. Porter?" Dragging himself from his thoughts, he stared at the man in front of him for several seconds before he could think where he was. "Mr. Porter? I'm Doctor Fitzpatrick. I've spoken to the police just now, and they told me that I could bring you up to date on your daughter's surgery." Randall sat up straighter in the chair and waited for the news. "She's in grave condition, I'm afraid, but I have hope that she'll pull out of this. Tisha is young and in very good health. While she's lost a great amount of blood and has had some pretty extensive wounds to her body, I think she stands a good chance of coming out of this with only a few adjustments on her part. Had she not been brought in when she had...? Well, I think that given what happened to her, she's very lucky that someone went to check on her."

"What happened to her?" Burt had come to stand beside him, and the doctor looked up at him. "I'm going to tell him whatever you tell me, so it will save me time if you just pretend that he's her father too. Burt is...well, he's her friend as well as honorary uncle. And doctor, we'd like it straight up like I like my bourbon, if you don't mind."

"All right then. She had been stabbed forty-three times in the chest and arms. Her legs have been cut as well, but I'm not sure with what just yet. The police have pictures of each wound and are looking for the weapons now. She's been shot twice, once in the back and once in her upper left thigh that broke bones, but luckily didn't hit any major arteries. I don't know the timeline of these wounds as I was working to save her life, but I can tell you that she was tortured over a few hours' time." Randal nodded, his heart needing just a moment to catch up until Burt put his hand on his shoulder. It was both reassuring and comforting to have this man so close to him. "There was blunt force trauma to her head, arms, and the bottom of her feet. I would say that whoever did this to her took their time, wanting her to suffer for some reason. Her left hand is broken pretty badly, and we may have to wire it back together later. Right now, I'm solely focused on getting her past the point of being critical. I'm not sure if we'll need to go back in later and replace bone with metal in her hand, but for now, we have her in a hard cast to prevent her from doing more damage."

"Any internal injuries?" The doctor nodded, then looked at him when Burt asked. "Was there brain damage? What?"

"There is no way to soften the way I tell you this. Her abdomen was crushed, pelvis broken, and the fallopian tube on the right side was destroyed. Her womb was injured as well, to the point where it had to be removed or risk infection. As for her brain, we don't yet know what sort of damage is there. After she wakes, if she does, we'll be able to better determine where to go after that."

Randall felt his body just go limp. The words 'if she does' were too much. His mind simply said this is too much, and he embraced the darkness where his little girl was safe in his dreams.

CHAPTER 2

Zach loved being on the tractor. He supposed that someday the joy of owning and working with it, might diminish, but right now he was having a blast. He glanced up, seeing something out of the corner of his eye, and paused in turning the big monster around. Zach had nearly three more acres to plow before he could call it a night. Turning off the motor when Darin came toward him, he didn't bother getting down.

"Aunt Georgie said to tell you that you have to eat sometime." Darin tossed a heavy bag at him. "There's water in there too. And so you know, I ate two of the cookies she sent you. Think of it as payment for coming out here."

Zach took out the thick sandwich and bit into it after getting it unwrapped. He was hungry and had really forgotten, again, to bring him out something to eat. The water was cold too, and felt good going down. When he polished off half the sandwich, he asked Darin what else was going on.

"Nothing. Not much anyhow. I did have some news for you on the permits, but I think you know." Zach said that Ed had been out earlier. "Yeah, thought so. Also, Emma is working on some sting shit that has to do with her office. It's going to go on a little longer than we had thought. Her

19

and Palmer are working up some kind of thing to get some answers."

"So long as she keeps safe, I don't care. That person, Beth, her assistant, she called the house this morning, asking me for money and telling me again that I'm not playing ball with the rest of them. I just let her go on about how I was really losing out by not doing what needed to be done in the first place." Darin asked him what that meant. "I asked her. She said that I'd learn to play by the rules sooner or later, and she wasn't into learning curves with me. Also, she told me again that so long as I'm using outside contractors, I am never going to get the permits to finish off Child Like. I think she's off her rocker."

Zach handed the cookies to his brother. He'd been eating less sweets lately, not for any reason other than he was trying to watch what he consumed. He could have used the extra calories, he supposed. Working like he was, he was burning more than he was taking in. Darin, of course, simply ate them all without a thought.

"Logan and Charlie aren't due back from their honeymoon for another week. And Emma is going to go away for a few days too, by the way. A buddy of hers from her childhood has been hurt pretty badly. Her dad, Randall Porter, asked her to come visit him if she could. Do you remember Porter any?" Zach said that he'd heard the name, but no, he'd not met him. "I remember him being around. The only reason we have that nice football stadium at the high school is because of him. And he put in that really nice playground set at the nursery school despite the fact that he has one at his own company. Keeps them both maintained too, I guess."

"This is his kid then?" Darin nodded. "What happened, do you know? Or has she just broken a nail and needs moral support from another woman?"

The moment the words left his mouth, he wanted to take them back. From the look on his brother's face, he knew it was bad. And when Darin turned his back to him for a moment, Zach told him he was sorry, it's just that he'd been so busy of late.

"I know. But I'm glad I told you about this and not Emma. This woman, she's like her sister without there being blood, you know what I mean?" Zach said that he did. "It's been all over the news. I'm assuming that you still don't have a television. A grade school blew up. I mean, from the looks of it, it was a huge fucking bomb. There is a crater now that you could park this sucker in and have plenty of room left over."

"She was in there?" Darin said that she'd been home, but they thought that her being hurt was connected somehow. "Christ. How bad is it? I mean, she's going to make it, right?"

"They're holding out hope that she will. Her name is Tisha. But anyway, she'd been stabbed like fifty times. Shot. Beaten, and then a blunt object, they think perhaps a sledgehammer, was used too. Whoever did this to her, they wanted her to suffer badly." Zach felt his cat stir over his skin. Women, all of them, were to be taken care of. "Emma leaves in the morning. And she's taking Emily with her. Mason is going to stay behind until the last of the steer are sold off, then he'll join her. He's asked Jace and me to keep an eye on the ranch for him, as well as a few other things. You'll help out too, right?"

"You know I will. This thing with Child, it's driving me crazy not to be able to get it finished up. I think some of the men have been going in late and working on it. Nothing where you could see it from the outside, but the interior is looking pretty good." Darin asked him how the house was

21

doing. "That's on hold for the moment. Not that it's bothering Beth, but I need to be there to pick out some carpet and stuff, and I've not been able to be there when the foreman is. I'll get it done eventually."

Darin left him a bit later. He asked him about the grain and how much longer it would be before it was ready to be taken into the barns, and Zach told him soon. He really wasn't sure right now. He was still learning. And when his foreman for the fields came out of the barn as he was pulling into it, he asked Billy Taggert the same thing.

"Corn can be used now should you want, but I'd put it in the dryer for a few weeks if you can. Horses and cattle both, they might like it better when it's damp, but they're not used to it and might get a belly ache from it. The hay, as you know, needs a few more weeks. While it's mature now, we want to give it as much time as we can on the stalk to dry out. That way we don't have any mold issues." Zach had known this, but it was nice to confirm what he thought. "You're doing a right fine job there, Zach. You keep this up and in a few more months, you won't need me."

"That isn't even funny. You leave and I'm done." They both laughed. "Did I tell you that I'm renting some land from Mason? He got those squatters off, and he is giving me a good deal on it to keep the land busy." Billy said that they might consider another tractor. "Yeah, I'm thinking on that too. But damn, this one nearly took me under. What with the house and stuff with it, I'm not making it too well until the grain is ready."

"You'll be doing fine in a couple of years. By then you'll have the land turned for the first time, and most of this tractor paid off. Buying another one, it's gonna save you much time in the long run, because two people working them can get you done twice as fast." It sounded obvious, but Zach knew that he meant that while one of them was plowing or whatever, the other could be readying the ground for the next planting. "You think on it. You got yourself a good deal on this one, and I'm betting the bank won't have any trouble lending you the money for the second one."

Going into his house, Zach tried not to think about how broke he was. He had the money in his account for Child Like from his brothers, and donations for the new building downtown, but that wasn't marked for this business, the farm. He was doing his damnedest to keep the money and what it was for as far apart as he could get them. He didn't want to get into a situation where he was borrowing from one account to pay the other.

To this day, he thought of that every time he thought he needed something. He left the money alone, never taking from one account to fill the need of the other ventures he had going on.

Dinner was a bunch of leftovers. All his brothers were married now, and Zach was always getting the remainders of this or that. Just two weeks ago, Holly, his sister-in-law, had brought a large casserole and some sealed up desserts. He pulled that from the fridge to reheat as he found the cold cuts that Susie had given him and homemade bread that Charlie had sent. He was having a feast tonight. But when someone knocked at his door just as he was sitting down, he was both glad and disappointed to see Landon there. The man would talk a person's arm off if he had the chance, and Zach was too tired to listen.

"I figured you'd be heating that dinner up again. Boy, you ever get anything fresh to eat?" Landon handed him a sealed bag of steaks in a dark marinade. "You go and put them on the grill now whilst I get rid of some of this mess. Damn it, boy, that casserole is nearly a week old. Time to toss it, if you ask me."

"I didn't. And it's two weeks old. Holly sent it over to me." He fired up the grill and talked to Landon while it got hot. "I don't have a lot of time to be cooking. I've about got things ready to go, and slacking now would cost me. Besides, it's not too bad if I put a lot of catsup on it."

"You ain't never slacked at nothing in your life. And that crap don't fix nothing, just buries the taste a bit." Zach tossed both steaks on the grill and realized that it had been awhile since he'd had a freshly cooked meal. Landon sat down on the deck chair that Zach had gotten from some estate sale and pulled out some papers. "I got me a proposition for you. Won't cost you but a little time, and I sure could use the company."

"Whatever it is, you know that I'd do it for you." Landon nodded, but didn't say anything else. "I heard that you've been house hunting. Are you having any luck with that?"

"Yeah. A little. Got my eye on this here place, but I've been told that it needs some work. Wasn't really thinking that I'd like to buy me a fixer upper at my age, but I'm thinking that I can find me a few guys to do that heavy work. That's what I'm here for." The steaks were done and Zach took them into the house. The picnic basket that he'd not noticed before was open now, and there were all kinds of delights to eat with the meat. "My Katie, she went by that new store there on Main and picked up some of their sides, seeing if they might be fit to eat for her shing-ding she's having later in the summer. We had us a couple of bites of some, but she was hoping that you'd tell her about these here."

"Sure." As he dished up the steaks, Landon got them some water glasses filled with ice. There was always a pitcher of water in the fridge, and he wasn't surprised when Landon pulled it out too. As the two of them sat down, Zach got them several spoons to do the tasting. "What sort of house is it you're looking at?"

"Katie, she's thinking small. I told her with the way you all are having babies, we'd need more than just us a bedroom and one spare. I don't care for that noodle crap, do you?" Zach tasted it and said it was too picklely for his taste. "So now we've changed our tune and we're looking for something a little bigger. Maybe a few more bedrooms and a bigger yard. You try that bean stuff, and I'll work on these here deviled eggs."

The conversation wasn't difficult to keep up with. Landon had been around them all enough that they knew how to understand the way his mind worked. So each time he asked him a question, then talked about the food, Zach easily answered him.

"The beans have sausage in them. I'm not sure I care for that. There is the pack lawn service that you could use for the yard, you know. Some of the high school kids are going to try and use it each summer to build up money for their senior trips." Landon asked him to get him information. "I will. What about the eggs? Keeper?"

"I like my Katie's better, but these will do in a pinch. You try them, tell me what you think." Zach ate one of them and said they were okay. But he did like the cole slaw…both of them did, as a matter of fact. "This here thing, what is that?"

"I think it's called bacon broccoli salad." Landon asked him if he was kidding. "No. I saw it on a menu once but didn't try it."

"Waste of good bacon if you ask me." Landon laughed. "Why would someone in their right mind want to go mixing broccoli, of all things, with bacon? Boggles the mind, I tell you, just boggles the mind."

He knew that eventually Landon would get back to the reason he was here. With his brother leaving, Zach was pretty sure that Landon would be over a little more. The man was a hoot as far as he was concerned, and Zach owed him more than he'd ever be able to pay back in friendship and kindness.

"I got me an eye on this house in town. Not in the best of shape, mind, but it's a big old mansion of a place that I'd like to be in for a spell." Zach asked him how much he'd paid for it. After a glare then a smile, Landon laughed. "We've been hanging out too much, I'm thinking. Yes, I bought it. Got it for a song and dance too. Needs some work on it. I had me this friend go over the foundation and all, and he said it's built solid. I'm needing a crew to come on in and pretty it up before I show it to my Katie. If that's what I end up doing with it. I got me an idea that I wanna run by you on that too."

"The crew I've been working with is Paddy's men. They're certified, most of them are anyway, and they do a good job. You should hire them." Landon nodded. "What else? As you said, I've been hanging around you enough to know when there's more to it than just you needing a renovation on a house."

"Want some pie? I'd like to get some pie." Landon stood up and started for the door. Zach followed, not sure what was going on, but again, figured they'd get to it. As they got in Landon's truck, Zach driving, he was worried about the old man. He loved him to pieces, but lately he seemed sort of distracted. "I think we'll head on over to the house when we've had us some pie."

The drive was made mostly in silence. Landon would say something that didn't require any kind of feedback from him, but he did try. Finally, they both gave up and parked in front of the diner. The sign out front proclaimed they had hot coffee and fresh pie. When Landon got out, he did as well. But instead of going in the diner, they moved down Main Street.

"This house, it's got all kinds of character." If it was the one they were standing in, Zach could see it was indeed a beauty. "I don't need the money, you see. I just have to have me something to do. A place I can putter around in and feel like I've done something that day."

"I'm sure that Mason loves having you around the ranch, Landon. If not, you can come on over and help me out. I'd even let you drive the tractor." Landon's excitement was there briefly, then gone, replaced by a profound sadness. "Tell me what it is, Landon. You're scaring me."

"Did I do the right thing, Zach? Do you think that I might should have done something different? Maybe been a little less...I don't know, done something to make it so that Dirk loved us?" Zach's heart broke for the man. "He wasn't ever like other kids. I mean, he'd have his good days, I guess, but mostly, he was just bad. Like something was so screwed up in his head that he just couldn't see what he was doing to the very people that gave him life."

"You remember what the doctor said, Landon. There was nothing you could have done differently to have helped him. He was that way because of something in his mind." Landon nodded and stared at the big house again. "Landon, tell me what's brought this on."

"You. Not that you've done a darn thing to hurt me. Nothing but a wonderful young man, you are. But I'm thinking that had I a son even half like you and your brothers, I might have died a happy man." Zach thanked him. "No need for that. Just telling you. But it got me to thinking, a dangerous thing for me, but I was thinking that I've no mark in this here world. I got me my little Emma, pride of my life she is, but she's not going to carry on my name. And at one time, the McBride name, it was something."

"It still is to a great many people." Landon asked him what would happen to it when he was gone. "You're thinking that once you pass on no one will remember you? Hell, Landon, you're like a father to me. I don't know what I would have done had you not taken me under your wing. But with that help, love grew. The kind I never got to have with my own dad. And there isn't a day that goes by that I don't think of you and Katie. Wonder what you'd think of what I was taking on. And none of that will change when you pass on. Which, I'm hoping, will be a long way off."

When Landon pulled out his hanky and blew his nose, Zach felt his heart twist up. He surely did love this man. As he dealt with his emotions, Zach made his way to the porch of the house. Giving the man time seemed the best thing right now, and he looked at the wide open wrap-around that needed a good scrubbing. When Landon joined him, he could see the man was in better spirits.

"Needs one of them swings. Not the plastic kind, but a good solid oak one. Might even work on that myself. I used to be handy with a saw or two." Zach asked him about the bushes out front. "Those have got to go. They can be mowed off, I'm thinking, and some pretty flowers for my Katie to fuss with put in out there. I'm picturing a nicer sidewalk too, I'm thinking."

"I love the gingerbread work here. Some of it might need to be replenished, but I know that there's this man in the pack that can take a good piece and make you a copy to do some replacements. And his brother does stained glass work." He looked at the broken but pretty mural over the front picture window. "I'm betting that at one time this would shine all through the front parlor."

They made their way into the house and Zach marveled at the knotty pine floors. The fireplace was solid marble, and the mantel was big enough to sit a person on it. A chandelier in the middle of the room looked like it had been there since the house was built. There were pocket doors, too, that still slid easily into the wall like they'd only just been built. But someone had painted them, making the oak that he knew was there look cheap and dirty.

"The kitchen is gonna need the most working over, I'm thinking. There is a big old stove in there that can probably be sold off as scrap, and maybe finance the whole darn thing for me." Zach looked at the stove and cautiously turned one of the gas burners on. "Well, I'll be hog washed and called pretty. It still works. Who would have thunk it?" Zach laughed.

"I'm betting you can get a pretty penny for this, Landon. And you're right, maybe enough to pay for at least some of the renovations in this place." The inspection on the house took a big turn when they surveyed the dining room. "Christ. You could feed all of us in this room and not have to worry about overcrowding. And look at the crown molding."

"You call that man, Paddy, up. You call him and ask him to have his crew come on out here and have a look-see at this here place." Zach nodded and pulled out his phone. To be honest, he was kind of excited too. When Jacob said he could be there in ten minutes, he and Landon waited, exploring the built-in cabinets in the oversized dining room. They were surprised to find china in them.

It took them nearly two hours to go over the house after Paddy and Jacob Welsh arrived. And at nearly midnight,

Jacob looked to be as interested in starting on the project as they were. They had not only found the china, which after a quick check on the internet turned out to be quite valuable, but they unearthed another fireplace, two stain glassed windows at the back of the house, and a room that, for whatever reason, had been boarded up and left untouched for years.

"You thinking that with these fix-ups, we can get more than we paid for it?" Zach asked him what he meant. "You know, flip it. I've been watching them shows on the idiot box, the television, and I see them people doing this all the time. Don't care for all the drama, but I'm thinking you and I can go into that."

"I think you could do really well at it. And Jacob's men could use the extra cash as well." Landon was shaking his head. "Or not. I don't know of a lot of construction crews around here, but I'm betting you can find one."

"Nah, that's not what I meant. I mean you and I go into business doing this. You being my partner in crime, so to speak. And my friend too. I know you got yourself a tidy little thing going with the feed and all, but I'm thinking you and I can have some fun at this." Zach wanted to, but there wasn't any way he could do this. "You and me, we could make these houses sure shine up."

"As much as I'd love to help you out with this, I don't have any investment money for this, Landon. I mean, I'll help you in any way I can, but being your partner, I just can't swing that." Landon only laughed. "Seriously. I'm in debt up to my eyeballs. I have more money going out than coming in at the moment, and to be honest, I don't think that's going to change anytime soon."

"You leave that part to me." Zach was afraid to ask him what that meant. "As of this here moment in time, you and me, we're going to do this. As partners. And if you turn me down, like I'm thinking you think you should, then you're going to have this old man sad as a man that has just found out that he has to eat that broccoli bacon crap for the rest of his life."

"That is a compelling argument, Landon, but I still don't have the money to invest with you." Landon said he wasn't worried about that, he'd do the investing, and over time, Zach could pay him back, just a bit at a time. "What if it fails?"

"Won't. Can't. I'm a McBride. You're a Douglas. It's written in the stars, my boy. This is going to be a great money maker." Another convincing argument, but it seemed that Landon wasn't finished just yet. "You need to go on and get you a realtor's license. That way, we don't have to pay them buzzards when we're ready to buy or sell."

"I'd be one of those buzzards, Landon." He smiled and said he was only joshing. "Okay, do you know how to get a license like this?"

The smile should have warned him. Zach should have run in the other direction fast and far. He just knew this was going to be trouble.

Chapter 3

Six weeks. It had been an entire six weeks since she'd been hurt, and Tisha felt no better now than she had when.... Well, that wasn't entirely true. She could move around in the wheelchair she had. There was the fact that she could eat semi-solid foods now. Plus, she was out of the hospital. It had only been two days, but she was home now, living with her dad as she recovered.

"Hello, princess. How are you today?" She looked at her dad and wondered what he'd say if she asked him once again to put her away. The nursing home that she'd looked into while in the hospital had very good ratings for caring for the broken. "Don't. I know what you're thinking, and I don't want to hear it. I want you here. I need you here."

"I know, Dad, but I'm also sure that you have a lot more things to do than to sit around with me all day, reminding me to take my pills and eat. Dad, this is not the way you should be spending all your time." He took her hand in his, careful of the bruising that was still there, and kissed it. "Dad, please. This can't be good on your heart either, worrying about me all the time."

"You think you being in that home would make me worry any less? Honey, I'd be there every day too. Reminding you to eat and take your pills. Besides, I'd rather be doing this for you than to be sitting over your grave every moment of every day wondering what I could have done to prevent that attack." He kissed her hand again. "Seeing you after the surgery, after that monster hurt my baby.... I need you here, Tisha. I need to know that you're safe."

Nodding, she decided not to bring it up again. He was right. She could have died. Tisha rolled her chair forward only to have her dad take over by pushing her to the kitchen. He asked her what she had on the horizon today, like she had a real life.

"I'm going to physical therapy at ten. Then I have this hot date for lunch." He patted her head when he had her pushed up to the dining room table. "I'm trying to decide if I want mashed potatoes again, or should I go all out and have two colors of Jell-O for dessert."

"I think two. And you're supposed to make notes on what makes you feel sick as you eat it. Ice cream, that's a no-no for now." She shivered when she thought of how sick the heavy creamed dessert had made her. "I should have started with something lighter, like a cheaper brand, and not gone for that one. I guess that it being made with heavy cream is what got you. I'm sorry, darling, but I'm learning too."

They both avoided the news now, and the paper. Alex was still out there, and to date no one had any news on where she was. But they were following the trail of trouble she was causing. Just last week she'd killed another teacher at the school, and had robbed a convenience store for cash. Tisha thought about the day she'd found Alex in her kitchen after hearing something fall over in her house. Before she could even enter her kitchen, a room that she hated more now that Alex had burst into her home, a blow to her head had knocked her to the floor, and Alex hadn't stopped hurting her.

"You were supposed to open that box." Alex had come out of nowhere, her shadow rolling over her like a dark cloud in the sky in summer. Then she saw it, saw what she'd been hit with…a sledgehammer. And there was a gun as well. Several knives had been laid out in front of Alex, like she was about to perform surgery on Tisha…which she supposed she had, in a way. There was also a long thick chain. And every piece of her weaponry, all of it, she'd used on Tisha.

Someone touched her arm, bringing her from her memories but not what she was feeling. Jerking away from the touch, not thinking about the pain it might cause her, Tisha tried her best to focus on the face in front of her, not the memories that had brought her to this point.

"Tisha?" She looked at her dad and tried to bring her fear and terror under control again. "Tisha, honey, she's not going to touch you again. I promise you this. We're going to find her and bring an end to this."

Breathing in her nose and out her mouth slowly, she nodded at her dad. In and out, the therapist had told her. In with the good, out with the bad. It helped with the pain as well. In with thoughts of goodwill, out with the pain and bad thoughts. Sometimes it worked, others, like now, it did not.

"I'm all right now. I promise. And I know that you're going to protect me." But she didn't, and she was pretty sure that her dad knew how she felt. Alex had been a friend. Not a good one, not even close, but they were friendly. Tisha would never have thought she would do any of the things that she'd done in the last two months. "It's just hard, you know? To know that she's still out there, causing all this to happen."

"I know, love. I know. But as I said, she won't ever be able to touch you again. I promise you this." She knew her dad honestly believed that, however, he'd not seen her, not seen her face. But her dad was a man of his word and it meant a great deal to not just her, but to a lot of other people. "Before I forget, Emma is coming by this evening to see you. She said that she has a surprise for you. That girl, I tell you, she's just a ray of sunshine, isn't she?"

"I would never have believed her to take on being mayor of this town. I know that I've not lived here in a while, but I can see what kind of differences she's made already. Did you see the way some of the older houses are being brought up to code and sold off? I'm telling you now, if I could, Dad, I'd want to tour all of them, and not just online."

She'd not told her dad, not just yet anyway, but she was looking long term now. A house…she wanted her own place and she wanted a yard. It would be a little while before she could do much in it, but it was coming up on fall and there wasn't a lot to do right now anyway. But soon, the doctor told her, she'd be able to shed this chair and walk with the assistance of a cane, but at least she'd be upright, not like she was now. Her mind skirted away from all the things he'd told her.

After she was loaded up into the car to go to her therapy, she pulled out her list of things she wanted to do while in town. As much as she wanted to go to the house she'd been inquiring about, it wasn't the time for her to tell her dad. Instead, she told him she was going to head to the mall afterwards because she had things to get in the way of clothing.

"Burt can go with you."

There wasn't any point in arguing with him, really. But honestly, she liked having the big panther close. Man or beast, she knew that he'd keep her safe. Tisha still had moments where she was sure she could see Alex in every face she saw.

"I have one meeting that I have to attend today. Then I'll meet you someplace and we can have some lunch."

After being helped back into her chair when they arrived at the doctor, her dad told her he'd send the car back for her. That was another thing she missed a great deal, being able to come and go as she pleased. Looking up at Burt, she asked him if he was ready for this.

"No, miss. I am not. I know that they're helping you, I understand that, but my heart cannot get around the fact that they hurt you as well. If you don't mind, after I check out the room, I'd like to wait in the lobby." She nodded, smiling at the huge tender hearted man. "Your father, he loves you... you know that, don't you?"

"Of course." She eyed him as they waited to be called back. "Why would you say that? What's he done now?"

"Done? Nothing that any other father wouldn't." She asked again what that meant. "There are people looking for that woman...you're aware of that, correct? Well, he has his own men working as well. He wishes to find her first."

"Will he?" Burt only shrugged. "He'll have her killed, won't he? Dad will take out his own sort of justice when he finds her by himself."

"I would imagine. When the doctor told him what had happened to you, it was difficult for him to embrace. His heart couldn't accept that someone hurt you and he'd not been able to protect you. It depressed him. Now? Well, now that he's had time to see that you're going to recover, he's gotten angry." It was like the stages of grief, she supposed. Much like she was going through right now with all the things going on in her life and body.

"Do you think him angry enough to carry out his own form of trial and jury?" Burt shrugged again. "I don't want him to go to prison for this. Is there anything I can do to stop him?"

"What do you think?" No, there would be no stopping him. Once her father set his mind to something, it was as good as done. And she loved him for it. "As I said, he loves you. Very much. But I also wanted you to know that no one and nothing will harm you again, so long as I live."

~~~

Zach pulled out the envelope and looked at it. He'd taken his boards ten days ago, and this was all that was left for him to do was pass. He was terrified to open the envelope, and with good reason. He didn't want to disappoint anyone.

Getting to this point, the point of no return he'd been calling it, had been difficult. He was a good student, that wasn't it, but with all the other things going on in his life, he'd had some moments when he wanted to just chuck the whole thing. Like two days before the test.

He'd been bringing in what would have been the first of many crops. As he was entering the barn—his mind not on what he was doing, but the stupid notes that were blasting in his ears via the recorder he had—he hit the side of the barn.

It hadn't been that bad. Not as bad as it could have been, he supposed. Zach hadn't been going all that fast, drifting really, but it was done in the front of every single member of his family. And they'd gotten the biggest kick out of it that he'd ever seen. Instead of laughing it off, as he should have done, he'd shifted in midair and gone after his brothers, and had gotten the shit knocked out of him in the process.

Zach knew it wasn't the barn. Nor was it the laughter from them, but stress, pure and simple. He was doing too much and it hit him hard. It had taken a broken wrist, four broken ribs, and more cuts than he'd been able to see to bring home the fact that he couldn't do it. And then his Aunt Georgie was there.

"You done?" He said nothing, his cat laying on the ground, defeated. "I want you to change back, dress, and come in the house. And if you try and sneak off and go home, so help me, Zachery, I will hunt you down and beat you to within an inch of your life." He glanced up at her, ready to argue, but he saw that look. One that he'd not seen in all his life, at least not directed at him. She was pissed off, and rightly so.

As soon as he entered the dining room, he nearly turned and left. But his brothers and their wives stood up, all of them, and looked ready to finish what they hadn't in the yard. Even Landon and Katie were there to be a part of his humiliation, he thought. Sitting in the only open chair, he hung his head, knowing that he was done.

"You feel better now that you've had your ass handed to you?" He nodded at Mason. "Look at me, Zach. I want to see your face."

"I'm finished. I was stupid and I'm done." He asked him finished with what. "Everything. I'm in over my head. I'm exhausted, and I hurt in more places than I can even remember having on my body. Not from today…I deserved that, I know. But I'm just not doing that well on anything."

"Finally." He looked over at Landon when he spoke. "Been telling you for two weeks to get you some help. You kept right on telling me that you had it. Well, even a fool could see that you had nothing. You're burning that candle at both ends, and right split down the middle too. What you trying to do, boy, die at a young age?"

He felt his anger shoot through the roof at Landon's words, but held on to his temper. It was getting harder and harder all the time to just be around them, much less have a conversation. Right now he wanted to lash out at his friend and tell him he was a part of the problem. He wasn't, but it was easier to blame someone else than to realize he was a failure.

"I took on these responsibilities on my own and I needed to get them done. I should have realized sooner that I'm not nearly as smart as others think I might be." Aunt Georgie asked him what responsibilities he had that were that important that they needed his undivided attention. "The shelter. The houses and the work on them. Beth driving me crazy with the permits and money that she wants to get the men working again. Then there is the grain and the farm work. I'm only going part-time at the university now. The classes that I'm taking aren't hard, but I don't have a lot of time to study like I should. I'm just.... I don't know if I can do this anymore. Like you said, I'm burning up too fast from everything. I'm losing it all."

"You lost it weeks ago if you think you can keep this up." He looked at Mason to argue. "Don't even try to say that you haven't. You're working too much and too hard. Any or all of us would have dropped anything to come to your aid. But you turned us down."

"I have it handled." They all shook their heads, and he could feel his temper getting the better of him again. "All right, so you've made your point. Are we done here?"

"We're not done. Not even close to it. Tomorrow morning I'm going to come over and learn how to drive the tractor. Then when you think I have it, you're going to go with Landon to look at a house. Not work on it, but look. After that, you're going to have a decent meal with your family —"

"I'm not four years old." Emma told him not to act like he was then. "Look, I've taken on too much. I'll just get better organized about things."

"No, you're going to get some help, and we're going to help you with it. We're family, Zach, it's how we get things done." Emma continued as he started breathing the way he'd been told to do before speaking, a way to get his words in order and not confrontational. "I've got Beth handled. Had I not gone into labor, she would have been gone long ago. But now that I'm going back in a couple of weeks, I'll be able to take care of this. Not just for you, but for everyone that comes to see me. You let me handle that bitch, all right?"

Zach wanted to tell her that he had it, that he had it under control, but he knew that they'd not listen to him, and they'd continue to treat him like he was a child.

He wanted to lash out at them all, tell them that he was doing just fine, when he looked over at Katie. She was the only one that hadn't said a word to him during this entire lynching. Or at least that's what it felt like to him. As he stared at her, she got up and moved to him as the rest of them left the room.

"Do you want to die?" He shook his head. "Have you in your head that you can do a better job all by yourself than you could with the help of the others? Perhaps you think they'll fail you? I'm thinking that you're not nearly as dumb as you think believe you are, but a man with a good, too good, of a sense of responsibility. Just like my Landon. So, what do you think, Zach, do you feel we'd fail you if you gave us a chance?"

"No, I don't think that." He was almost afraid to tell her what he'd been thinking. But he also knew that of all the people here, she'd be the one that would understand him. "They have families. Jobs that mean something to each of them. They...I have my fields, but we both know that they

41

only buy my crops from me because I'm their brother."

"Do they? I suppose you could be right. I'm sure if you had an inferior product, they'd go ahead and feed it to their animals, regardless of whether or not they got sick or died. That's what family does." He felt foolish and his temper rose again. "But then again, they could know, just as I overheard Mason tell Landon, that you have not only the best prices they've ever had, but a product far superior to any that they've used before."

"See, I am doing a good job. By working hard and getting the job done." She asked him at what cost. "I need to make a name for myself. I need...I need to prove to them that I'm just as good as they are."

It was out there now. His biggest fear. That he was, and he felt this deep in his heart, not nearly as good as them. He was just a farmer with barely enough money to pay for what he needed, much less the things that he would like to have.

"Do you suppose that when Landon and I were first married that I thought him a fool for spending all our hard earned cash on a ranch that he no more knew anything about running than I did? I didn't. I thought him brave, smart, and a man that I could depend on to not only take chances, but one that would work his hardest in keeping us safe and provided for. You are just like him." She took his hand in hers and continued. "He loves you. Sees himself in you a great deal. A man who's not afraid of taking a risk, which you know it was for you to leave the nest, so to speak, and become something different than a rancher. You knew not one thing about grains and hay. Nothing at all about tractors or getting a good deal on one. This project with the shelter? You saw a need and moved in a way to make sure that it was taken care of, another great risk to yourself. Then there are the houses. My goodness, I

42

walked through the one that the two of you are working on, and I nearly begged him to let us live in it. It's far and away better than any I've seen to date. And according to Landon, the two of you have contracted to do six more. Oh, Zach, you are far from being a failure. You've become a man to reckon with. A man of value in a great many areas."

"I don't know about all that. But the houses, it's fun. Hard work and expensive, but fun. I'm not contributing much to that part of it, but I'm working on it." She nodded and squeezed his hand. "What did you mean when you asked me if I wanted to die, Katie?"

"You are a young man, strong and smart, but you're overworking yourself, aren't you? How much weight have you lost, Zach? Twenty? Twenty-five in the last few weeks? You're not resting enough either, are you? Nor are you eating properly. I think if Landon didn't bring you food once in a while, you'd not be eating a single decent meal at all, would you?" He pulled his shirt from his belly. He had lost a lot of weight, and had taken to cinching his belt as tightly as he could just to keep his pants on. "You're going to have a massive heart attack if you keep this up. It will either kill you, which would hurt me profoundly, or it will put you in a position that will have your family not just doing for you, but you will not be able to do a thing for yourself at all. You will be confined to a wheelchair or worse. Just because you thought that you were invincible. That's a terrible way to hurt us, you getting injured and ill simply because you didn't want our help when you needed it. Don't you think?"

He sat there long after she left him. Zach had thought about not just what she'd said, but what she'd not said to him. Katie was disappointed in him. And he was pretty sure that had hurt him more than anything. After that and over the last

43

few weeks, he'd not only asked for help when he was in over his head, and that was a lot of times, but Katie had agreed to help him study for his realtor's exam.

Zach looked around at his family and wondered why he'd been so incredibly stupid to not have them help him. Not that he didn't have days where he would get to the end of it and realize that had he gotten help, he might have accomplished more, but he was learning. And it was a big learning curve he was on.

"Are you eating or just going to stare at us?" He looked at Susie when she hugged him to her. "I have it on good authority that the baked beans are better than that crap at the deli, and the cole slaw is just good, but not great."

"Landon." She nodded at him. "He and I were taste testers for some of the things that Katie brought in. I think she'd do a better job with a blindfold on with some of them, but then, I got free food out of it and was happy to help. By the way, don't try the broccoli bacon salad if she went that way. According to Landon, and I have to agree, if even bacon can't make it good, there's no hope for it." They both laughed as they made their way to the buffet table. "What is this all about anyway? Just a way to get us all together?"

"I think she needed this more than anything. Tomorrow would have been Dirk's birthday, and I think this is her way of dealing with it." Zach hadn't known that and was sorry for it. "I can't imagine what they're going through, can you? I mean to have your own son try and kill you would be hard enough, but the way that Dirk acted about everything must have about broken them all."

Dirk had been Landon and Katie's only son. He'd been.... Well, to say that he'd not been right in the head would have been grossly understating it. Dirk had been horrible, taking what he felt should have been his and making demands on two of the nicest people Zach knew for no other reason than Dirk thought he was entitled. To everything. And it didn't matter who he had to hurt or kill to get it.

He filled his plate and sat down next to Katie. As casually as he could, he shoved the still unopened envelope under her plate. Picking it up, she asked him if he'd read it yet. Shaking his head, he told her he was afraid to. Standing up, she made an announcement while holding onto his test results.

"Excuse me, everyone. I would like to read you a letter for the state boards." He tried to pull her back to her seat. With a small tap to his hand, she opened the letter. "Congratulations, Mr. Douglas—"

They all started yelling and clapping at those three simple words. He was stunned. Not only that, but when she got to the results of his test, a perfect score, he couldn't believe it. He'd passed. He was a realtor. Holy Christ, he'd done it. He stood too when his family finally quieted down.

"I think I owe you all a great apology." Mason asked him what he'd done now. "Nothing. I mean, I've done plenty, but this, this right here, I couldn't have done it without all of you. And I know what you're thinking, you still don't believe it. But you guys, my family, you made me see that I can do just about anything I want, so long as you're right there behind me kicking me in the ass."

His aunt cleared her throat but said nothing. Zach told her he was sorry. He could tell that neither of them believed he was, but he smiled at her, giving her his most charming smile of all. After that, the party was bigger, louder, and more fun for all of them.

On his way home, he stopped by the first house that he and Landon were working on. In two days he would have an open house and hopefully they'd sell it. It was going to make someone very happy. Going inside, he turned on the lights to see what had been set up to display the place.

The kitchen, of course, was his favorite room. The appliances were all new and state of the art. The big stove had earned them a pretty penny, and they'd used that money to buy décor, something they could use in all the houses if they needed to dress them up a bit.

The kitchen table had been salvaged and cleaned up from an auction. The chairs, the same place. Cabinets were plentiful, high in places that they could make them, and also a great many of them low enough for anyone to reach. Even the bar in the room had been set with some bar stools that he was sure had come from an actual bar. He'd found the dishes for it himself, getting an entire box of them for just a buck.

Zach moved to the big dining room. The walls, once they had taken down some of the ugliest paper he'd ever seen, had been beautiful. And after adding some salvaged wainscoting from another part of the house, it gave the room something they'd not expected...a homey feel that was functional at the same time. It was still hard for him to believe that it had only needed a good scrubbing and a coat of varnish to make it look this good.

They'd had to replace two of the windows in this room, and had gone to the local high school to see if they could get the pattern in the front door duplicated in those windows for the dining area. Zach thought they'd turned out really well. And it had helped a few kids show off their talents.

The floors were all hardwood that had been discovered under layers of not just carpet, but linoleum as well. Again, just a good cleaning was needed, and a sander run over them to bring out the lovely pattern of the wood. He loved the warm feeling it gave both here and the living room. He entered the latter now.

The fireplace had been saved, which he and Landon had had their doubts about when construction had begun. But with a little work from a couple of his brothers, not only had they got it working again, but the mantle had come out better than he'd imagined it would. All the rooms, he thought as he made his way up the stairs, had turned out beautifully.

There had been five bedrooms on this floor when they'd started out, but only one bathroom. After a few days of tearing out a couple of walls and reworking the rooms, they'd ended up with four nice sized rooms as well as two baths, one for the master suite. They had also found a large ornate elevator that went from the basement to the upper levels.

After making sure that everything was ready in the house, he made his way home. Tomorrow he had a lot of crap to get done to free himself up for the open house, but he felt that he'd get it done. And he had people to cover for him if he didn't. But instead of going into the house, as he should have, he supposed, he stripped down and shifted to his cat. He'd been neglected too of late.

CHAPTER 4

Getting around with a cane wasn't all it was cracked up to be. Plus, it didn't take Tisha long to realize she was pushing herself again. But she wanted to take a look at this house more than she'd wanted anything in a while. So instead of doing what she knew she should have, like resting, she and Burt made their way to the big antebellum house.

"Want me to go in, and take some pictures and send them out to you?" She glared at the man who had been her constant partner since they'd left the house that morning. At his laugh, she wanted to take her cane to his head. "You're looking a little green around the neckline, miss. Just do me a favor and sit here and rest. I won't say a word to your dad if you do that."

"You won't anyway." He said nothing. "I need to make plans, Burt. You understand this, don't you?"

"I do. I really do. But these plans will be for nothing if you overdo it and end up back at the hospital." She knew this as well. "Rest. I'll see if they have a drink or two, and we'll go from there."

When he went inside the house, she watched two couples come out. They were talking about the house. How beautiful it looked and that they couldn't believe how much young

Douglas had grown up. She listened to them, trying hard not to appear so as one of the couples described not just the house, but the kitchen.

"I love the countertops the most. And did you see that stove? I could cook such a big meal there." The man with the woman asked her if she even knew how to cook. "Yes. I just don't care to cook for the two of us. But that house, doesn't it just scream entertaining?"

"No. What I got from it is comfort. In every room on every floor. The bathroom with the clawfoot tub was perfect, the stand alone shower big enough to share. And that fireplace? Man, whoever worked on it, they loved their job." The entertaining lady asked him what he meant. "The eye for detail. The wood in the room is perfect, even with all its imperfections."

"Perfect imperfections? That is the stupidest thing I've ever heard." As they moved off the big porch and to their cars, she knew she needed to see this house more than ever. As soon as Burt came out with a glass of iced water, she knew he was impressed with what he'd seen as well.

She told him to tell her about it. "You're not going to want to leave here unless you make an offer. I kid you not, miss. This house is so full of beauty, you're going to love it. I do too. And the kitchen is a dream...even you, who can't boil water, will love it."

As they made their way into the front entrance, she fell in love. The flooring, parquet oak, met them with a bright shine, and the cherry pieces that danced around the room made the entire area seem welcoming and inviting. They made their way deeper into the room just as a couple was entering where she thought the kitchen was. A woman met her at the doorway to a large open living area.

"Hi, I'm Susie Douglas. I'm helping my brother-in-law show the house. I don't think he figured this many people would show up." Burt asked her how many they thought had come through. "Over two hundred. I know that a lot of them just wanted to look around, but the interest in buying the house is outstanding. And for good reason."

As Susie told them about all the work that had gone into the room they were in, Tisha looked around. The tin ceiling had been painted to match the crown molding; the floors, knotted pine, were polished to a nice flat glaze. Even the furniture, period pieces that had been well cared for, made a person want to not just sit down and kick off their shoes, but to snuggle up on the couch with someone special. Tisha turned away from that thought. There would be no one like that in her life.

The dining room was huge. The built in cabinets would hold a lot of dishes, and big windows let the afternoon light shine in and brighten the room. The lighting, small and well placed, would make the room beautiful even on the cloudiest of days. She ran her hand over the large plank table and felt like she was stepping back in time, to a place that was well before her age, but no less wonderful to her.

The stairwell to the upper levels was left untouched by her. She wanted to go up, needed to see the master suite she knew was there, the bed with the four posters that someone had picked out with her in mind, but she wasn't able to manage it.

"You can use the elevator." Tisha looked at Susie, almost afraid to ask her if she was kidding. "When they started the renovations to the house, no one even knew it was back there. Someone had hidden it behind a false wall, and when it was uncovered, not only were they able to restore its original beauty, but managed to get it working again too. Mason and Jace worked for two days on it. They're the tinkers of the family."

"Oh, Douglas. You're related to Emma." Susie grinned and said that she was. "I completely forgot her married name until you mentioned her husband. I never met him, but.... I'm Tisha Porter. My dad is Randall Porter."

"Yes, she talks about you all the time." Tisha assured her that it was probably all true. "I hope so. I'm so glad to meet you. Are you looking for a home here in town again? Emma said that you've been staying with your dad."

"I have, and yes, I'm very interested in this house. I remember it as a child. I was never invited in. I think they thought that Emma and I would vandalize the place if we were allowed in. We were not the most well behaved little girls." Tisha laughed at her own memories. "I'd very much like to see the rest of the house, if you don't mind."

"Yes. That would be.... Look, here is the man of the hour now. Zach, this is Emma's friend, Tisha. Tisha, this is Zach Douglas, the realtor, as well as someone directly responsible for the beauty of this home."

Burt stepped in front of her, too close, and growled. She had no idea why, but she found herself falling backward, and if not for the quick thinking of Susie, she was sure she might have landed on her ass. Susie helped her to a chair, but before she could ask Burt what the hell he was thinking, he was backed against the wall by the younger man and held a good foot off the floor with a hand around his throat. Tisha just stared. Burt was not a small man. Tisha started to stand but Susie held her back.

"Don't move. If you do, one or both of them are going to get hurt. And you might as well. Just let them come to terms with this." She asked Susie what was going on. "Just give them a minute or blood will be shed in your new home."

A big man came into the room and stood behind Zach, who was holding Burt. It surprised her to no end that her friend didn't pull his gun and shoot the man, but he was calm, not even fighting the hand that held him. The second man standing behind Zach, speaking calming and slowly to him, kept glancing her way. She wasn't sure, but she thought he might think this was her fault. It wasn't until Zach let Burt go that she let out the long breath.

"What the hell are you doing?" Both Burt and Zach looked at her. Tisha wasn't sure which one she was yelling at, but she'd been afraid and there was no way they were going to do this without some sort of explanation. "I want the two of you to back off, and one of you explain to me what brought out this beast in you."

The stranger laughed, then Burt grinned. It was the strangest thing she'd ever witnessed. And when Susie started to laugh too, Tisha decided that she'd had enough and stood up. The only person who wasn't laughing was Zach, but he had the strangest look on his face.

"Don't." She paused when Susie spoke. "You're only going to piss him off, and I'd not do that right now."

"Who?" They both turned to the group of men, and she knew she meant Zach. Without taking her eyes off him, she spoke to Susie again. "He looks...I was going to say mad, but that's not it. He looks like he could.... Is he a shifter?"

"Yes. Cougar. Burt, I'm sure you know, is a cat too, but a panther." Tisha nodded and stood up, leaning heavily on her cane. "You're his mate."

"No." Tisha turned to look at Susie and shook her head. "No. I can't be. Not that I have anything against shifters or them finding their mates, but it can't be me. I don't have...I'm not going to be anyone's mate or wife, ever."

Zach moved toward her. He was slow, his body moving like the cat that she knew now that he was. He never touched her, but he was close enough that she could see the golden flecks in his brown eyes. The tawny color of his hair that just peeked from the top of his shirt. When he reached out, his finger just a breath away from touching her cheek, Tisha thought about moving, backing away from it, but she couldn't. His touch, it seemed, was what she needed more than she needed to breathe.

~~~

Zach could see her fear. And her need to understand. He could almost taste her uncertainty as well. But the need to touch her, just to see if she was real, made his cat rub along his skin. When she took a small step back from him, he wrapped his arm around her to keep her from leaving him.

"Let me go." He wanted to do as she asked, demanded really, but he found that he liked having her in his arms. "Please, you need to let me go. I can't be what you need."

"Why not?" He heard his brother talking in the other room, rounding people up to give them a moment or two. "Would you like to see the upper levels? I heard Susie tell you that we have a way to get you there."

"No. I want to go home." He mentioned how there were four bedrooms and two big baths, one of them with a clawfoot tub. "Don't do this. You have no idea...I can't be your mate. I'm not well."

"I can see that." He pulled her along with him, moving them toward the back of the room where the gilded elevator was. "The elevator was put in when the original owner of the house had a stroke. It was to help him get up and down the floors without assistance. One of the maids who worked here during that time period said that Mr. Grant, the man who lived here, was very nasty and hated when people thought him to be less of a man. The stroke, you see, disabled him quite badly."

He opened the doors and helped Tisha inside before closing the door behind him. Pressing the button that would get them moving, he was careful not to get too close to her. The enclosure was large, more than big enough to fit a wheelchair, but it had been designed to hold a hospital bed when Mr. Grant's health was at its worst, Zach told her.

He babbled on about the history that they'd gathered on the house. The people who had worked here, most of them in their late eighties, had more to add. As Zach helped her from the elevator, he showed her the work they'd done on the long hallway.

"Landon, my partner and good friend, said that to leave some of the original colors would appeal to the masses. I just liked it because it was warm looking. The wood in this area of the house had to be redone…the place where the elevator was put in wasn't sealed well on the roof, and there was water damage." She touched her fingers to the dark paper and smiled at him. He loved the color of it with the white wainscoting at the bottom. "You like this, wait until you see the master bath."

"I love the tile here in the hall. I would have thought carpet, but this is so much better." He told her it had once been covered by carpet, but they thought that it had been taken up because of the wheelchair. "I can see that. It would be harder on a carpet with a chair. I was in one recently. Well, I still use it when I've had a particularly hard day."

"You look tired now." She felt tired too, like she had run

for a long time and the exercise was just catching up to her. After leading her to one of the benches that they'd gotten really inexpensively, he sat beside her but far enough away not to spook her. "You know what I am, what sort of cat I am."

"Yes. Burt, he's a panther and has been around me my whole life. I want you to know that I don't have anything against you, not personally, but I can't be your mate. Not with what's happened to me." He asked her what she thought that might mean to him. "Plenty. I...I don't know if Emma told you or not, but I was recently hurt pretty badly by a woman. I'm not sure why she did what she did — she's still out there — but there are two more teachers that taught where I did that have been killed."

"Emma only said that you'd been hurt. I believe she went to visit you while you were in the other hospital." Tisha nodded. "This woman, she still looking for you, do you think?"

"Yes. I mean, I really don't know because I don't know what prompted her to do this in the first.... I can't have children. Not ever. She damaged a lot of my insides when she took a hammer to me. I'm lucky to be alive, I know that, but I can't ever have children because of her actions."

Zach said nothing. It wasn't something he'd ever thought about, having children, but he could see where it would bother her. A woman who taught children, he would think, would want some of her own. Instead of talking to her about it, telling her his thoughts, he leaned back on the bench.

"My brothers have children. Not all of them are biological. Mason and Emma have a daughter. Jace and Holly have a new baby boy. My brother Darin, he and Mercedes are going to have one too, and they have Bonnie, Mercedes's daughter.

You'll get to meet them. And just so you know, Bonnie is young, ten now, but she has met her mate in Patrick. He's a wolf. Actually, so is she. There was a fight and she nearly died, so she was converted to save her life. My sister-in-law, Susie, you met her, she has this amazing ability with horses. Well, all animals, and some people too." Tisha said nothing but didn't leave him either, so he was encouraged. "Logan, my other brother, he is married to Charlie. They own and run the winery at the other end of town. And then there's my Aunt Georgie, who met her mate recently, and her and Palmer are married now too."

"So many people." He nodded and grinned at her. "You have six brothers, five sisters-in-law, and a lot of extended family, it sounds like. You're very lucky. I just have my dad, Randall, and Burt. There are others, I guess. The staff and all, but for the most part, it's just been the three of us." He got up when she did. "I'd really like to see the bathroom. I have a real fondness for big homey bathrooms."

Taking his cues from her, he walked down the hall with her. Her steps were sure but slow. She was losing energy, and he could see it in the way she moved and spoke. She talked about the wallpaper, the glass door knobs on the rooms they passed, as well as the old frames that held some of the art that they'd found to go in the house. As he took her through the master bedroom to the bath, he saw her eyeing the bed and he had to grin. She wasn't indifferent to him at all, he thought. Or she needed a nap. And as soon as he opened the bathroom door for her, he knew it was the latter of the two.

"Steady there." He picked her up when she stumbled while going through the doorway. Carrying her out to the bed, he laid her gently on it. "Do you need something for pain?"

"No, I'm all right." She closed her eyes and he could see the tears falling now. "Yes, I need something for pain. It's in my purse in the car. I'll get it in a moment. I shouldn't have done this today. I need...I just needed normal."

Reaching for his brother, he asked him to send someone for her purse. He pulled the large wing backed chair closer to the bed. Taking her hand in his, he held it while she lay there crying, and his heart hurt for her.

"Susie is bringing your purse up to you with a glass of tea. Burt told her that you have to eat something light with it, so she's also bringing you a few cookies, all right?" She nodded and asked him if she'd passed out. It took Zach a few seconds to realize what she was asking him. "No, I can talk to my family without you knowing. I'm sorry, I should have said that. Burt would like to know, through asking Jace, if you'd like for him to call your father."

"No. I just need a minute." Zack told his brother as she continued. "You must think I'm a fool for doing this. I was just going to come here, see the house, and leave. Make an offer if I liked it, but I never meant for me to be up and around this much."

"I understand. For the past few weeks, I've been taking on more than I should as well. It took my family to knock me in the head a few times before I got it. Not to lessen that your injuries are more physically and mentally draining, but I understand about feeling the need to do it all sooner than you should."

The knock at the door had him going to it. He took the plate and the glass from Susie, and wondered aloud how the showing was going.

"Well. I think you might sell this sooner than you expected." She looked around him to Tisha. "I talked to

58

Emma a few minutes ago. She said that she'd explain to your dad that you're at her house and for him to not worry. Is that okay?"

"Yes. Thank you." After nodding to him, Susie left, closing the door behind her. Zach handed her the glass and the plate, which had a dozen cookies on it, as well as her pain pills still in the bottle. "I want this house."

"Okay." He would give her the world if that was what she wanted. "I know that Landon has plans of using the money from the sale of his house to finance the next three we're working on, but I'm betting I could work something out with him."

"I don't understand." He told her what they did, or what they were attempting to do. "You buy cheap, fix them up, and sell them? That's wonderful. How many other houses have you done so far?"

"This is the first one we've finished. And since I'm having my own house built now, I'm figuring out things to add and take away from my home as well. Like that tub you like so much. I have two in my house. The contractor wasn't thrilled about the changes, but he's made it work for me. And I've been to a lot of auctions and have been picking up things that I like, enjoy, or have no idea what I'm going to do with it but buy to add later. My barn is filling fast."

She took her medication and lay back. He could see the moment that it kicked in, taking her under. Instead of leaving her, as he should have to check on things downstairs, he sat with her. Watching her breathing without pain was wonderful. Zach was just dozing off too when Landon touched his mind.

You found her. He told him he had but she was afraid. *Not of you. You're the sweetest kid I know. What's got her all twisted up? That woman?*

59

I don't know much about what happened to her. Do you? Landon said that he did, as a matter of fact, he'd been talking to the police and Randall had given him the file on her when asked. *I'd like to see it too, or at least have someone talk to me about it. She said that she can't have any children, as if that's going to be a deal breaker for me.*

To some it would be. To her even, I'm betting. According to her dad, she's been wanting a houseful of little ones since she was a kid herself. Zach told him that it could still happen for her. *Yes, sir. I just knew you'd say that. Told my Katie just when I found out, you'd be good for her. Little Tisha, she's been given some hard knocks by this woman. Terrified out of her own skin most of the time, and her dad tells me that she has the worst kind of bad dreams you can imagine. He said that her screams will wake up the dead.*

He reached for her hand again, and taking it into his he could feel her relax. Zach watched her as Landon told him about the paperwork that he'd be sending over to him. Zach told him thanks, and then he explained about the house.

Never figured that we'd have any offers, much less from your own mate. Well, you should run her out to your house and show her that it's better than that one. I love what we've done to it, would give it to you as a wedding gift if she'd have it, but you show her your house. I'm betting that one there will be on the market again faster than a jackrabbit can take off. Zach laughed and asked him just how fast that was. *You should know that I can beat your bottom as quickly as I can hug the stuffing out of you. You behave now and take care of that little woman of yours. She needs it as much as you do.*

Zach told him that he would and closed the connection. After yawning three times in as many minutes, he decided that while the chair was nice, it wasn't big enough for his long legs. Stretching, he moved to the other side of the bed, and pulled the pillows off and tossed them to the floor on the side where she was resting. After throwing the lap blanket on the floor, he lay down. Covering his face with his hat, Zach told himself that he just needed a little nap. It was the last thing he remembered as his mind closed down and his body drifted off.

CHAPTER 5

Alex crept through the house and paused in front of the kitchen doorway. She'd been through here three times in the last forty-five minutes, and was surprised to find someone in the kitchen this time. The man standing here, a big hulking guy, didn't scare her, but she didn't want to encounter him either. Waiting him out seemed the best course of action.

She was doing the Lord's work. Every time she took care of a sinner, she knew she was that much closer to being with him and all his glory. He'd told her, over and over, that she had to do this, and now that she was acting on his words, he was rewarding her daily. Just today, he'd given her a van to drive around in instead of having to walk everywhere. She could also sleep in it, which gave her time to pray to her Lord without anyone interrupting her.

The man in the kitchen was on his cell phone. She could hear him speaking, telling someone that they needed to get home quickly as he was ready to leave again. Alex knew it was time for her to move to a place that she could do her work when Melly, a teacher that had sinned at the school, came home. Wherever she had been, Alex knew she was sinning. That was what she'd been told about them, they were all monsters and sinners.

Going to the stairs in the sublevels of the house, Alex pulled out one of the sandwiches she'd made herself today when she'd been alone in the house. Her Lord had told her that it would be a long wait, but she would be rewarded if she would do as instructed. She was also to make sure that she was well hydrated as well as nourished. She remembered his words like she did her own name.

You cannot do my work if you are ill, my child. Eat well and make sure that your water is as pure as your thoughts. She told him that she would. *I will give you so many riches once you have completed my work.* And that was what she was doing here today.

The house was nice, much nicer than the other three she'd been in lately, but none of them compared to the one that Tisha had been whoring in. The sinner had been selling herself for such a big house, she'd been told. It was one of the reasons she'd been told to end her life with suffering.

Tisha had been hard to hurt. She knew that her responsibility had been to end her life, but she'd not been able to do that. Alex had thought that she had killed Tisha and told the Lord this. Alex had left her for dead but had been wrong. The Lord pointed out that because of Alex's laziness, the whore lived. She had taken better care after that to make sure that her job was finished before leaving the houses.

Alex thought of the first time that her Lord had called to her. She'd been in bed with a man, having the best sex she'd ever had, when the man just dropped. As she struggled to get free from him, Alex realized that he had bled all over her and the bed.

When she'd finally gotten out from under him, her body was covered in warm, fresh blood. Alex had screamed only once, barely getting out the sound before she was told to shut up. The man, she forgot his name now, had turned his head all the way around from his body and glanced at her. He looked as if he'd been broken, then his head put on backwards. It nearly made her sick to see him lying there like he'd been. But then he spoke to her, scaring the shit right out of her.

I have a need for such a woman as you. Not saying a word, Alex only stared at the body all twisted up like it was. *You have been called upon to come into my fold and help me with ridding the world of teachers that are whores and liars. You will be my chosen one.*

"I don't understand." The body had gotten up from her bed and stood looking down at her. His ass, the first thing that she'd noticed about him in the bar that night, was right in front of her face, his head still turned so that he was able to see her. "How is it that you're making your head turn all the way around like that? Doesn't it hurt or something?"

This body has no meaning to me. I can do what I wish. And I wish for you to help me with the whores of the world. She tried to think if she knew any, and the first name that popped into her head was Tisha. *Yes, she is the one. You will need to take them out of my world so that they cannot harm others with their sin. The others, the women, the whores that you work with, will also need to be taken from this world. I wish them dead for what they have done.*

She thought about Tisha and her coming into work every day with new shoes on and pretty dresses. She had the best of everything. And her room was the nicest too, with all the bright pictures and posters, the new crayons that she handed out like they were free. Alex even hated that she had a new car too, and when her dad was in town, he would take them all out to eat, like he was trying to buy them or something. But Alex had never seen her dating anyone, and if she had, she didn't talk about it at school. Then the week before classes began, Tisha had done something bad to her.

"I have some extra things that are left over from my class last year. I'd like for you to take them if you want." Alex had asked her what sort of things. "Well, crayons for one. I know that kids can go through them pretty quickly. Someone donates them to me every year, and I have more than enough for this new one coming up. They're all new and still in the boxes."

She was giving her castoffs, Alex had thought, and not the new ones she said. Used and broken up crayons that the children wouldn't want. But instead of telling her no, Alex thanked her. Then Tisha doubled her crime by laughing and adding insult to injury.

"Also, I was wondering if you'd like to have the mats that the kids didn't use last year that are still packaged up. I know that they're supposed to provide them, the children's parents, but there are so many families that have little to no money that I buy them up so I can help out. Would you like those too?" More castoffs, more things that would be used up and broken. Before Alex could tell her no, that she'd rather die than take them, Tisha continued. "I have a lot of boxes coming in too. When they do, I'll give you everything that I can't use, and we can have the best rooms possible. Don't you just love the first day of school when all the kids are as excited as we are?"

"No, I do not. You think I can't have the best room without your help?" She'd been harsh, mean, and she could tell that Tisha had been shocked. "I can do just fine on my own, Miss Porter. You just go on ahead and decorate your room like a crayon factory exploded, and I'll do mine in a way that doesn't distract from what I'm trying to teach them."

"I never meant that, Alex. I was just trying to be friendly.

I thought we were friends."

Alex told her she was wrong and hung up. And then the Lord had come to her and told her to take her out of this world. He also told her what she had to do to rid the world of women like Tisha Porter and her nasty ways.

There are pages where you can find links to make what you will need. I want you to find a way to take them all from this world at once. I wish for them to be taken care of soon, the first day of classes at that whorehouse called a school. She got up and went to her computer immediately. *You will do this for me, my child, and I will reward you greatly.*

After doing as she was told, they made plans to make it work. She had less than a week, only a short amount of time to get things in place and to please her Lord. Then there was the matter of the man's body.

His death had been necessary. It was the way of things, the Lord told her. One must be willing to die for the betterment of the world. He'd taken the man's life so that he could speak to her freely. The knife lying on the bed where they'd been, he said, was the murder weapon. And that she had to not just get rid of it, but the man as well, for it would have her prints on it. When asked why, he explained.

I had to use you to rid yourself of him. As I have said, I need you to come into my fold and do my work for me. I have a list, not long, but one that I would like for you to take care of for me. And if you do this correctly, which I've no doubt that you will, then I shall reward you greatly. He'd said that to her before, and Alex asked him if it was money. *Nay, my child, you will have no use for money when you have me in your heart.*

The bomb was easy to make. She'd just gone to the sites on her computer that the Lord had told her to. Making a list, she bought the items easily enough, even going so far as to travel out of town to purchase a few of them when the Lord suggested it.

After getting all the things she'd needed and putting it together, he told her that while there would be a lot of innocent lives taken, it would be a good thing, that his word was law. After that, he assigned her to make twelve other, smaller bombs to be set off when Tisha was dead.

She will come in to her room and see the big package on the desk. It will be like her to open it when there are children there. To show off what was inside. As soon as she opens it, she will be stricken from my list, and those others that work there as well. Alex asked him about the children again. *You dare to question what I have set before you? I do not need for you to do this if at every turn you are going to ask me about my actions. Are you going to do as I need?*

"Yes, my Lord. I am but your humble servant."

It was only a matter of taking in all the smaller bombs and setting them about in the areas that he told her, then taking in the larger box and setting it on the desk the afternoon before school was to start. Alex was excited, very much so, and sat up to watch the television all night so she'd not miss a single bit of coverage when they were all dead the next morning. But it didn't happen the way it had been told to her.

The news reports came in about ten that night. The building was gone. A gas leak had taken out not just the building, but cars and the playground equipment as well. No mention of Tisha, nor of the other sinners that worked there. The only bodies that they'd been able to find so far were a few men that worked to scrub up after the nasty children were gone for the day. Alex had failed her Lord.

You will need to go and finish my work. She nodded, hearing the Lord speak to her as if he were in the room with her now. *Go to her home and kill her. I will tell you what you will need to*

*bring with you to finish the job. You have failed me, Alexandra. I'm
terribly disappointed in you.*

"I'm so sorry. I will take care of this now." Going to the
garage as he told her, she gathered what he said she'd need
and made her way to Tisha's house. The list of things needed
was long; hammer, nail gun, a knife that she'd taken from her
kitchen, tape to bind her with, and a gun. She put that in her
pocket and took all the other items to the car.

It had taken Alex several hours to do all the things that
her Lord had told her to do. She'd broken in and attacked the
woman even as she begged for her life. Alex had decided that
she'd do this sort of work for the Lord whenever he asked
her. She'd enjoyed upholding his laws. And making Tisha
suffer had given her the biggest thrill of her life. But she didn't
mention that to the Lord. She felt he'd find it wrong of her.

The door to the basement brought her from her thoughts.
The light flared on, and then the door shut loudly in the space
she was hidden in. Pressing her back to the wall behind her,
she watched as the feet touched each step, the body of the
person taking up more and more space as he entered her area.
It was the man again, his body bigger than Melly's.

Melly was a fifth-grade teacher. She was old, nearly sixty,
and didn't strike her as the wanton type. She taught Sunday
classes and had pictures of her grandchildren all over her
desk. Alex had had a hard time thinking of her as a whore,
but her Lord would know best. And it was her duty to take
her out of his world. Alex was startled out of her thoughts
again when the man spoke.

"I don't see it." His voice sounded like he was angry; it
was then that she realized that he was still on his phone. "I'm
looking at the washer right now, Melly, and I don't see your
blouse. Could it be in the dryer, or even in our room?"

Alex could hear something, a buzzing sound that she knew was Melly answering the man. He moved closer to the washer and the Lord spoke to her again. He seemed angry for some reason, and it made her react quickly.

Kill him. She moved forward and hit the man as hard as she could with the hammer to the back of his head. When he dropped to the floor, the Lord spoke again. *Hit him. Kill him. He's a whore's servant. Kill him.*

Hitting him several more times, closing her eyes when his head simply fell into itself, she stepped back when the Lord told her enough. Her body was slick with blood and sweat, and she rubbed it all over her arms and face. It was like having a spa day after a long work week. She was glad now that the Lord had told her to do this as she was born, naked, to do this, and it felt wonderful. And it made it much easier to clean up. Her clothing wasn't covered in the whore's blood.

Shower here. Get all the blood off your body before the whore comes home. She will hurry now, knowing that something happened to her servant. Alex picked up the phone, hearing Melly screaming out the name of David. *When you are cleaned of his vile blood, we shall have to leave here for now. But not too far, for she will come back.*

Alex did as she was told, even taking her hammer into the basement stall with her. When she was finished, she walked naked over to her duffle bag and pulled out her clothing to dress. Her back to the body, she didn't bother to check to see if he was dead. She was getting very good at her job for her Lord, and knew that she'd ended his sinful life.

Barefoot, she made her way to the shower again and poured the drain cleaner that the Lord had told her to purchase just for this purpose after her work. Then she picked up things that might lead the police to finding her before her work was done. He'd told her several times to be careful of that, for if she was caught now, they'd not let her continue on with her work for him. They would want to put her on a pedestal and whores would fear her.

Tonight she would need to find her a place to sleep, then tomorrow, if the Lord saw fit, Alex would come back here and finish the job. So much to do. But he promised her she'd get to kill the biggest whore of all, Tisha Porter, if she continued to do the good job that she was. Alex was going to make it her mission in life to be the best servant of her Lord that he could find.

~~~

Harlan knew just what they were going to find here. Nothing. There would be no residue from the killer, no weapon left behind, nor would anyone find a single print that they could use. It was like this woman had some sort of special powers to clean herself from every aspect of the crimes she committed. They all knew who it was, but attaching her to any of the murders so far would be impossible in a court of law. He looked over at Melody Harrison as she spoke to one of his officers.

"We were on the phone and I was asking him to bring me my favorite blouse. My husband has been so good about making this thing safe for us. He only stopped by here because I asked him to. My poor husband, David. Whatever will I do without him now? I just don't know why someone would kill him like this." She held onto the tissue in her hand like it was a lifeline. "We were talking about where I might have put my blouse, when suddenly I heard this cry of pain from him. I asked him what he'd done, what he'd hit, but there was no answer. He'd been after me for months to get the basement cleaned out. I promised him I would have a huge garage sale right after school started. I told him that we'd use the money from it to have a nice little vacation with the grandkids. Then I could hear it."

"Hear what?" He asked her again when she only stared at him. "You said you heard it. What was it you heard, Mrs. Harrison? Someone talking, perhaps?"

"No. Just the pounding noise. Like.... He had a power hammer, one of those that just zips the nail into the wall?" Harlan told her what it was. "Yes, an electric nail gun. It sounded like that. Sort of a pop-pop-pop, but much louder."

She must have realized in that moment what she'd been hearing and burst into loud sobs. He didn't blame her. He'd seen her husband in the basement. He might have been just as sickened by the sound seeing what the murderer had done to the older man.

His head was gone. Not that it had been removed, no, that might have been easier to take. But it had been crushed in with something hard and heavy. Harlan wondered what sort of strength it might have taken to not just take down a man that size, but to kill him this way too. He was sure that they'd be finding brain and skull fragments for years, if not for as long as the house stood there.

"Sir?" Harlan looked at the officer that had arrived first on the scene. He was still slightly green, but he was upright now and not puking in the yard. "They found something downstairs. Could you come on down and have a look before we move it?"

He'd have to walk by the body again, he knew it. And while he wasn't the squeamish type, seeing the devastation done to the man was hard for even a seasoned officer like him. Nodding once, he made his way to the basement and around the body to stand in front of the shower. It took him several seconds to see what the man was showing him.

"Is that it?" The officer said that he had no idea, but it did fit what the Porter woman had told them. "Bag it up and then tag it as evidence, and take it in personally to have it looked at. Do not let that out of your sight for any reason."

"Yes, sir. But there's something else." He pointed this time, directing his attention to the bottle on the floor of the shower. It was hidden behind the curtain, and well out of sight of his first walkthrough of the area. "I'm thinking that this is why we never find anything in the house. She takes care of it before she goes."

They were the first true pieces of evidence they'd had in all this time. Something that might connect Alexandra Grace to the murder spree. He hoped to Christ this was her hammer and bottle of drain cleaner. Even if they found a partial print on either of them, a spot of DNA, he would feel that they were making progress. More than they were now, just cleaning up the dead bodies and chasing their asses. The city was running scared, not having a positive idea who might be doing this.

Again with instructions on not to leave the evidence in the hands of someone else, he sent the officer off. Making his way around the room, Harlan looked at it with fresher eyes. If she left this behind, perhaps she'd done the same with something else, possibly bigger. Holy shit, he thought with a grin, they might have the murder weapon.

It took them an extra five hours to go over the house again. They found evidence that she'd made herself a sandwich as she stood waiting for her victim. The small crumbs, like the hammer, might have gone unnoticed but for the small piece of plastic that stuck from one of the steps.

She'd taken the time to not just make a meal, but to wrap it in the plastic wrap that was in the drawer of the house. They found several prints on the inside handle of the refrigerator. A glass in the sink that had a good set of prints on it as well. Harlan thought that they were hitting a gold mine. But they still had no idea why she was killing the people that she worked with.

Harlan tried to think what would be going through her mind as she stood there, waiting at the bottom of the stairs for her next victim and quietly eating her ham on rye. He wondered if she was naked. It would stand to reason, he supposed. There was no clothing left at the scene that they'd been able to find, nor did any show up in any of the dumpsters. But then she'd been pretty meticulous. Taking what she brought and leaving not one single thing in the house...until now.

By the time he was home, he'd gotten the call on the prints. The prints did not belong to anyone in the household. The police were, at this moment, running them against the ones that had been discovered on the knife at Alex's house. He shivered whenever he thought of what they'd found at the home of the murderer two months ago.

He was aware that what she'd done to the body had been done postmortem, but it made it no less sickening. The arms and legs had been cut off the torso into what he assumed were manageable pieces for her, then dumped in the trash can on her lot. While there was no real experience in her cutting, it was done with a steady hand, the coroner told him, without hesitation in any of the cuts.

Harlan had since figured out she was looking for her signature. The body of Carl Winter, a deadbeat father of six who had apparently picked Alex up at a bar, had his neck broken. Not just broken, but his entire head had been twisted around so that it faced backward. When they'd found him, it wasn't easy to determine if he'd had sex or not until they found his DNA in her bed. The condom that he'd worn had been removed and not recovered.

But since then, even with Tisha, she'd been using blunt force trauma to maim and eventually kill. Harlan figured that Alex had decided on a hammer to the head as her mode of dispatching teachers and anyone else in the house. It was easy to carry, he supposed, as well as hide, and she was getting really good with it. The monster that she was becoming would be hard to stop.

He looked up at the notes he used at home. It was just a huge pin board that he'd use when he couldn't make the dots connect while he was working. The pictures of Tisha were there, all of the teachers that were on a contact sheet, each picture no more than an inch by an inch. But he had no trouble seeing them. He'd been there and knew each and every wound, bloodied place, and cut on each body.

"Alex, what were you thinking?" He'd asked himself that several times over the last months. Six teachers, all of them dead. Two spouses as well, their bodies just as mangled and beaten as their other halves. "Why would you, someone that had been a teacher for more than twenty-five years, never having any issues, do this? You have no reprimands, nothing. Why would you suddenly decide not only to blow a school up, more than likely when it was full of children and teachers, but seemingly want to finish what you started? Were the teachers the intended all along? Will you go for the children next?"

Harlan didn't think so. When she'd killed the fifth-grade teacher and her husband two weeks ago, there had been children in the house. One of them, a third-grader at the same school, lay sleeping in the other room. He had no idea why, but Harlan thought it was the teachers. But for what reason?

From all accounts, Alex was a nice person if a little abrupt at times. She had a problem with her landlord on occasion, but nothing too serious. Her parents were both dead, no siblings that they could find. But her students from the last year had mentioned that she'd talk to herself. A lot. Of the two or so dozen that had been interviewed, more than half of them said she also faded out, sort of sleeping with her eyes open.

Harlan stared at the woman's picture that was also her ID photo. If he'd had her as a teacher, he might have been slightly afraid of her, he thought. When asked, none of his own kids had anything nice to say about her either. His son, Harlan Junior, a college student now, had told him that she was nuts. And that had been over ten years ago.

"Do you talk to someone? Do you see things that others don't? Hear things?" He had no idea. Then he thought about the conversation that Tisha had told him about. The one that she'd had with the woman weeks before all this had happened. The crayons.

Tisha had told him that she'd only been offering Alex some of the items that she'd had donated. The younger woman had solicited the help of friends in higher places, and had more than enough supplies and simply meant to share her bounty. She'd done it every year since she'd been at the school, and all the teachers had taken the supplies. Except for Alex. She never took anything, so Tisha had called her to tell her what she had left.

"She acted as if I had offended her in some way. That I was offering her...I don't know, like I was trying to pawn off things that were inferior or something. I told her they were new, still in the package." Harlan asked her then if she'd said anything to her while she'd been in her home. "Yes. She called me a whore."

Harlan got up and went to his wall. Whore? He thought

about the way the women had been killed. The men too that had been in the houses. It was the work of something personal. She'd killed these women because...she believed they were whores.

She was ridding the place, the school, of whores.

The more he thought of that, the more clues seemed to come into place. While the papers knew that the victims had been killed by blunt force trauma to the head, they didn't know that each of them had also been beaten in their groin region. The abdomen and vagina had been crushed. They thought that Alex had killed them, then stood over them and beaten them between the legs repeatedly. She was destroying them and their sex because they were whores. But why come to that conclusion?

He might not have the answer to that now, but he had a feeling he was on the right track. For whatever reason, and criminals didn't really have to have a sane reason to do something, Alex was killing these people because she thought of them as whores. He wondered, not for the first time, if this was her first killing spree.

CHAPTER 6

"I'm going to have to kill you, Tisha. You've been selling yourself to others long enough." Tisha tried to run then, but she wasn't able to...her legs were hurting, her body was heavy. "I've been sent here to do the Lord's work, I was sent to rid the world of your kind."

Tisha felt her fear double, the colors in the room she was in were too bright. Alex had broken in and was going to murder her. Dragging herself across the floor, she felt the bite of the hammer again, this time in her back. Screaming for someone to help her, Tisha felt her hair being jerked back, the knife at her throat.

"I have you." She fought the arms around her, hitting and screaming to be set free. "I have you. No one is going to hurt you."

The words meant nothing to her. Alex was going to kill her. Tisha tried to free herself, the tight bind around her was strangling her, she thought. Tisha didn't want to die.

"Tisha, wake up." The sting to her face made her fight harder. The second time she was hit, her eyes opened and she saw the man. A man was holding her, not Alex. Alex wasn't there. Grabbing onto who she now knew was Zach, she held him, sobbing into his shoulder.

"She wanted to kill me." She felt herself being lifted up and found herself on his lap, being held like she was a small child. "Whore. She kept telling me I was a whore, and that the Lord had told her that I needed to die."

"I've had my brothers call the police. I want you to tell me everything you remember. All right?" She nodded and heard him say something low. Burt...she knew that he was there and that Zach was talking to him. "Okay, love, I have my phone on and it's going to record what you say. Just let it tumble out."

She told him everything she remembered. The feel of the hammer hitting her. The way that Alex kept saying that the Lord had sent her. That all of them needed to be dead. How Alex had hit her over and over, telling her that it wasn't her idea, that the Lord had sent her.

"I didn't do anything to her." He said he knew that. "She stood over me at the end, with the hammer raised up high, when she suddenly got this look on her face, like she had no idea what she was doing. It was then that I noticed that she was completely naked. Why would she take her clothing off to come to my house?"

Zach said nothing, but told her to go on. Tisha spoke of what had happened, telling him things that she'd only just thought of...the look on Alex's face, the way the hammer that she'd used was huge, not like one she had in her own toolbox. Zach explained to her what it was.

"She hit me with that thing over and over, whatever it was called." With him holding her this way, close to his body, Tisha felt safe, like she could tell him what had happened and not feel the fear of it overpowering her. "I had spoken to her a couple of weeks before. She has been a teacher for a while, I'm not sure how long, but her room—she teaches third-grade—

has nothing in it. A free calendar that she gets from the bank, I think, a writing chart above her chalkboard that is out of date. As well as her carpet, the one that the children are to sit on, is worn in a lot of places and needed to be replaced when the school did upgrades a few years ago. I know that she could have gotten a new one, but for some reason, she didn't."

"I don't know much about this, other than the few things that I've caught from my brothers. I don't own a television or listen to much music, so I don't get a lot of news. But I have to tell you, sweetheart, she sounds off her noodle." Tisha laughed. He sounded so sincere, so honest in his opinion, that it made her feel good for some reason. "You better now?"

"Yes, I think so." The words that had been said to her that day, the pain of the hammer and the gun that had been used on her, faded away somewhat. "I'm sorry that I freaked out. I have terrible nightmares still."

"I'm very sorry that I hit you." Zach ran his fingers down her cheek to her lips. "If you really want me to feel better about all this, you should kiss me to make it all better."

"But you hit me. Shouldn't you be kissing me?" The thought of his mouth on hers, his tongue sliding along hers, it was a wonderful thought. "Zach, am I really your mate?"

"No. You're more than that...you're my everything." He moved closer, his head lowering to hers. "My brother, Jace, is downstairs and just told me that the police are here. He came to the house when he felt I was terrified out of my mind for you. Kiss me, Tisha. Kiss me before they come up."

The touching of their mouths was warm, soft, and almost too gentle for her. But as soon as he slipped his tongue into her mouth, touched his to hers, she felt heated. He pulled her closer, shifted her on his lap so that her breasts were pressed against his chest. And the deeper the kiss went, the more his tongue dueled with hers, the more she found that she wanted. Wrapping both her arms around his shoulders, careful of her hand, Tisha wanted everything he seemed to be promising her in his kiss. And when he lifted his head, she whimpered.

"Oh love, you have no idea how much I'd like to lay you back on this bed and take you. Strip you down one article of clothing at a time until you're bare for me to look at, to feast upon." She told him yes, please. "They're here. They want to talk to you. And as much as I'd like to tell them to go away and fuck off, we need to get this woman caught and out of our lives."

She knew he was right. It didn't make her want him any less, but he was right, the police needed to be aware of what she'd remembered. When he sat her back on the bed, then got up to move, she watched him adjust his cock. Christ, he was huge. She licked her lips without thinking about what she was doing.

"Don't look at me like that, or I'm locking the door and telling them to go the fuck away." She nodded, then shook her head. "Honey, I kid you not, right now I could free my cock and come all over you."

"We don't know each other all that well. I'm not saying that I don't want you, but it's scary how much I don't care about that right now." He just laughed…it was hard, and not with humor. "I don't know why we're doing this. We can't be mates, you know that, right?"

"We are mates, Tisha. We've already started the process of it. I nipped your flesh, tasted your blood." She felt the burn on her neck when he looked there. "I did it in passion. I really didn't mean to. Well, that's not true, I did, but I'm not sorry that I did."

"I can't have children. I might not ever be able to walk

again without a limp. That woman, who I thought was my friend, she destroyed everything about me." Zach moved so quickly that it took her breath away. And before she could say anything, he had her picked up off the bed and into his arms. "Please."

"She didn't destroy anything about you. You're strong or you'd not be here. You could have easily given up, let her take your life, but you fought her with all that you are and survived. You're a survivor, Tisha." He kissed her then, not soft or gentle this time, but hungry, brutal almost. When he lifted his head from hers, she stared into the most beautiful eyes she'd ever seen. "You can't have children? Well, big deal. I don't care about that so long as you're in my life. There are millions upon millions of little ones out there that don't have parents. We can't take them all, but we can certainly make a difference in the lives of a few if you wish."

"They won't be yours." He asked her why not. "Because I can't give you one of your body. I won't be able to give you a child of your own."

"Any child that we bring into our house will be a child of our own. Maybe not of our blood, but that won't matter a hill of beans to them or us if we love them. And we will. You not being able to have a child from your own body is tragic, I don't mean to make it sound as if it's not, but it will never lessen my love for you. Never make me feel that you are anything but the perfect person for me. And I will never feel anything for you but love, simple love, for the greatest treasure a man could ever hope to have."

She was still crying when the police and a man that had to be Zach's brother came in. As they moved around the room, adjusting chairs to suit them, getting out notepads and recorders, she thought of Zach.

He said that it mattered little to him about children. But she knew that he was wrong. Every man wanted a child of his own. She looked at him now, how he joked with Jace, and the way he kept looking at her, devouring her without touching her. It was then that she came to the realization that this man wasn't like anyone she'd ever met before. He was.... Well, he was scary, but in a good way.

"Miss Porter, I'd like to talk to you about what you might have remembered." Zach told them about the taping of her story, and let them listen to the words that scared her even now. "Good, good, this is extremely helpful. Now that we've listened to it, we have a few more questions for you. Are you up to it?"

She looked at Zach as she answered. "I want her gone from my life so that I can move on with mine. I have a lot to think on, plenty, but I want to do so without fear of her coming for me. And I think she will." At his nod, she felt like she could go on, could deal with this, and when it was over, she was going to be able to figure out what this man meant to her, if anything. And see if it could be long-term.

~~~

"They're making a killing off those old houses I told you months ago had to go." Beth watched her father-in-law just lay there. "Did you hear me? I said that those men are making money off those houses that should have been put on the destroy list last year. You were supposed to make sure they were down."

"You're not blaming this on me. I told you years ago that you needed to make up a contract and have it signed off on by the old mayor. That way it would have been us that decided what needed to be worked on. Not to mention being the city's contractors in all works. As it is right now, we got shit to use to show that we're the ones in charge and able to simply skip over the bidding wars and just get paid when they come up. Right now, if I were to go to Miss High and Mighty with a suggestion these places were unfit, she'd only go behind my back and have all of them looked over by this other crew. They're making us look bad, Beth. Really bad. I thought you had them stopped, anyway." She wanted to brain him. Just pick up a nice brick and bash his head in. But she couldn't. They needed each other. Or so she had thought years ago. Now.... "Come on over here, Beth, and suck me off again. Christ, you do that like a pro."

"You're not listening to me." She watched him fist his cock. The man had some moves on him, but she wanted him to get things going in the right direction before they were caught fucking around. Literally. "Don't do that. You're distracting me from what I want."

"Come here and let me give you want you want. You know you like it too." That was the trouble, she liked it too much. "Suck me, Bethy. Come on and let me fuck that mouth of yours."

Before she could think it was a rotten idea, she made her way to him. The man could and would make her scream more than his son did on his best days. And her husband never gave her anything like she wanted. Fuck her then roll over and sleep. That was his idea of making love.

When Joe sat up on the edge of the bed and held his cock out for her, she got down on her knees in front of him. Licking at the drips of precum on the dark tip, she looked up at him. Lately, she'd been noticing that he was really getting fat and old. But now wasn't the time to think about that.

"You make me crazy." He nodded and moaned when she took him in her mouth. Cupping his balls in her hand, she

85

slid him in and out of her with a bob of her head. Reaching down to the floor, Beth pulled the vibrator out of her purse and turned it on. Nothing could get her wetter than hearing that thing buzz.

Putting it to her pussy, she felt the small climax take her. It was only the beginning; the real release would happen when she pulled from his cock and let him come all over her. Christ, nothing ever made her climax any harder than knowing that when he was empty, he'd toss her to the floor and eat her.

"That's it, baby. You make me come and I'll give you your own release. You know you'll love it." Moaning, he grabbed a handful of her hair and jerked her harder down over him. "Swallow, Beth. Swallow me down. Make me come, baby."

She did as he commanded, the urge to gag never bothering her because they'd done this so many times that it was easy. And when he began to raise his hips up, meeting each of her downward strokes, she pressed the vibrator harder to her clit and screamed around his cock. He came hard, pulling free of her mouth just as his cum sprayed her in the face.

Beth rubbed it onto her face, her breasts, and belly. Even as he threw her back on the floor, her head hitting hard against the carpet, she felt her pussy soak. She was ready, right now, she needed to come like this. The moment he bit down on her clit, she came. Beth came hard even as disappointment washed over her. It wasn't the way she wanted it, and he had to know that.

Joe moved off her, his body slick with sweat, and she noticed that it was looking sort of old around his cock too. He still had a better dick than his son and knew how to use it, but he was looking old and very undesirable lately. She was sure it was the hormones creeping up on her. That, along with his inability to do as they had planned made her snappish.

"That's it? You get what you want and I'm left hanging?" He told her she'd come. "Yes, but once. You know I like to come four or five times when you do that."

"I just don't have it in me today." He hadn't two days ago either, and one time before that. "Look, if you need more then use that cock on a stick. I'm telling you right now, it's going to be more enjoyable than I can be with you harping on me all the time."

"Harping? Harping? I do not harp. I'm trying to get this thing done so we can get out of this town and be together." She watched him pull his pants up over his tighty whities that hadn't been tight or white in a while. "Joe, have you lost weight?"

"Yeah. Anna, she's pissed at me again and has not been cooking. And you know how much I hate eating out." He sat down. "I'm sorry, babe. Next time, I'll make it up to you next time. Now, tell me about this building you were talking about. What are they doing to them that makes you so upset?"

"They took the Burner mansion and revamped it. Tore out walls, redid the kitchen. I went over there a couple of times, pretending to check on permits, and it looked really good. And yesterday, at the open house? They had over two hundred people show up. If they sell it for what I think it's worth, they'll make about fifty grand in profits." He leaned back in the chair and looked like he was thinking hard. "Can't you do that? Buy up a couple of houses and revamp them like they did? I was thinking we could take a couple of the lesser rundown ones and make them look that good by slapping some paint on the walls and hanging some pretty shit up. We'd be long gone before anyone found out that it wasn't done like the Douglas and McBride properties."

"I suppose we could. But there is the consideration of

paint and pictures. I only have this business on account'a my daddy left it to me. I can barely build something with blueprints. I mean, I can slap one together on the cheap, but as far as which wall needs to be taken out, who to call to get flooring done? That's not something I have any knowledge of. I can look into it for you, but I don't think that'll make the new mayor any happier with me. She's been trying to get me into her offices for over two months now about some outstanding contracts. Can't you get her off my back?" Beth told him she was trying, but she was like a dog with a bone. "Well, she's about to gnaw right through me to my bones the way she's going after me. Yesterday, I had to hide out for the better part of three hours while she had cops in the drive waiting on me. I know it was her, heard her tell them to wait me out. Fuck, good thing there was that accident on the main road or I'd be hauled in by now."

Beth hated Emma Douglas. The bitch had been a thorn in her side since they were younger. Beth hadn't helped matters at all, she supposed, by targeting the pretty little Emma McBride when she could, but then she'd gone away to boarding school. When she returned, she was.... Well, Emma had gotten a good deal smarter about a great many things, including how to use her fist.

"She's just trying to look good for the election." Not that she'd had to work all that hard at it. "I tried starting rumors about how she wasn't fit to take the duties of mayor when she got pregnant, but that didn't go over at all. People like her. I wish to Christ that her brother would have beaten her more as a kid. I think it might have made her a little easier for me to intimidate."

No, that wasn't right either. Even as a young kid, Emma had possessed the ability to see through her right to the bones.

There had never been a time when she'd been able to lie to her either, not when they were children. But now…well, now Beth had been practicing for a long time. She could convince you that it was raining outside if you were standing in the bright sun. Beth had a gift.

"The sooner you get her off my back, the better I can work things out to get us out of town. I can't pay that money back; you know that as well as I do. There ain't none of it left." He stood up and stretched. "It would be better for us all around if she were to be dead. And soon. I've been real lucky so far in not getting caught where she can find me, but that ain't gonna last much longer. And when she starts looking really deep into things, we're both going to be pretty fucked."

When he left her, Beth sat there on the floor and thought about what he'd said. He'd told her flat out to kill her boss. Not that Beth hadn't thought of it a million times a day, especially here lately, but damn it, how the hell was she supposed to do that? As it was now, she was doing everything on her own about keeping them in money and him out of jail.

Two weeks ago, Emma had pulled her into the office and asked her to get all the contracts that were outstanding on the Rogan Company. In addition to that, she wanted the amounts they were paid, how many of the jobs they'd finished, and if they were still working on them, what was the estimated finish date. Beth told her she'd get them, not that she'd have to look them up really. Beth knew each job and amount paid, as well as what had been done with the money when Joe's construction company had gotten the checks. It had gone to having fun.

But Emma was getting harder to fob off. Even harder to work for. Just the week before her spawn had been born, she'd pulled her into the office again and asked about her father-in-

89

law and where he was hiding out all the time.

"Joe is his own man. But you don't have to worry about the jobs he's won. He's doing the work like he said he would when he got the bids. He's a man of his word and works hard." Emma cocked a brow at her. She realized how bitchy she sounded. "What I mean is, his crew is working on each of the contracts that he's been awarded. I know that they've run into some issues, but they're working them out."

"Then I'll need a list of those issues as well." She wanted to tell her to fuck off, explain to her that it wasn't her concern, that she had it under control, but Emma had continued before she could. "Do you know who is in charge of choosing the person that gets the contract? I'd like to talk to them as well."

"Usually it's the mayor, but I was told to do it when the last guy was in office felt it was beneath him to pick a name off a list." Beth lifted her chin. "I think I've been doing a good job of it. The contracts don't lay on the desk anymore, and someone is finally working on things."

"Are they? I've yet to see a single person work on any of the projects I was told about. Last year there was to be a new playground put in at the park. So far as I can see, all that's been done to it is someone put up a sign saying that it's coming soon. I think *soon* was a little premature, don't you?" Beth had said nothing, sensing a trap. "I want you to give me each of the contracts to look over, as well as any unfinished jobs. I'm going to see how much work is done on each of them according to the time frame that they've had to work. There are deadlines on each of them...the work must be done within a certain timeframe. Right now, it looks as if he's defaulted on a few of them, if not all, of them. Wouldn't you say?"

"I don't know." She did know, right to the day, how far behind Joe had been. "Let me talk to him on a personal level.

Maybe I can get him to get his butt in gear." Emma had told her it was too late. "What does that mean?"

"That for the last few years, more probably, he's not done a single project that he took on. What I don't understand, and perhaps you can answer this, is why he keeps getting the bids when he obviously isn't qualified to do any of them." True, but Beth didn't want the bitch telling her that. "Have those reports like I asked for by the end of the week. And you should think about finding yourself someplace else to work, Beth. I'm thinking that when this all is out in the open, you're no longer going to be able to work here. Anyplace, for that matter, but I want you to turn in your notice within the next month."

As she left the office that day, all Beth had been able to think about was that she was going to be fired. And if she was, there would be no more contracts or money coming in for them. They depended on that cash; her and her husband, plus, Joe and her mother-in-law, all of them had come to enjoy the extras that her little business was bringing in. And now, because of Emma and her fucking rules, it was going to end.

It was then that she remembered the date. Christ, the bitch was coming back to work full-time next week, and she'd ask her again about the paperwork that Beth hadn't done. Emma having her kid when she did had given her a much needed break. But now it was time to figure out something else. Or kill her off as Joe had suggested.

"Damn it, I'm going to have to kill her so I can have my cake and eat it too." Beth got up and went to the bathroom. Looking in the mirror, she knew that she'd not be able to do it. Not anymore. "Life fucking sucks, you know that?" Her reflection, of course, had no reply.

She looked down at her flat belly. She'd have to tell her

husband soon that she was going to have a baby. If she told him at all. Joe was forcing her hand, and it depressed her a great deal. But Beth had no idea who the father was, either Joey, her husband, or her father-in-law, Joe, and that might be a problem down the road. At least if she kept it, she thought, she didn't have to worry about it not looking like the family.

But Joe was pissed off about her getting herself knocked up, as he called it. He'd told her when she mentioned that she might be that she'd fucking better have an escape plan if she was. He'd even said he'd pay for the abortion for her as cover for her with Joey. Cover for her. Like she'd trust him at all to do a damned thing anymore.

She wanted this child, but apparently her lover didn't, and that hurt her more than she could have thought it would. Joe had told her that she had to get rid of it, as if it were nothing more than a bag of trash. Or, he'd said, he'd do it.

Beth put her hand on her belly, not feeling anything but knowing that there was something there. Crying now, feeling so alone in the world, she turned on the shower to let the tears fall unchecked. Life now really did suck, she thought.

CHAPTER 7

The house looked pretty good, Zach thought. It still needed some work finished, but they were working on that when they could. He had all his appliances bought—they were in the big barn still in the boxes—and he had picked out the carpet colors a while back. He wondered if Tisha would want something different. He wondered, too, if it would be only the carpet that she wanted changed.

"Do you cook?" He told her he could make a good grilled cheese and ham, but nothing else. "So why did you put in this big kitchen? I mean, I hate to cook, and even I think this is really big."

"My family." She looked at him. "We hang out in the kitchen when we're all together. Last week we were at my aunt's house, and with us growing all the time—you know, adding more family to us—we barely fit in that one now. I thought when they come over, I wanted us to have room."

"You're all very big men." He nodded, thinking of the way she'd looked at his cock yesterday, and had to take a slow breath to calm his cat. "What kind of counters are you having put in?"

Counters? It took him a few seconds to get his head back on the subject at hand. "I had a hard time considering that.

I thought granite, but I heard that it's so overdone that it's sort of a standard now. I wanted different. So when we had the counters put in the Burner house, Jacob, my contractor, suggested we do concrete. I guess you can have it colored to match just about anything." She moved around the room, picking up the tile that he'd chosen before setting it back down. "If you don't like anything, we can have it changed. It's not up yet, so we can—"

"To be honest with you, Zach, I have no idea what I need to do. I feel...I guess you could say I feel really lost right now." He didn't say that he did too, but waited on her. "I thought you were just showing me this house because you built it. Do you really want me to move into your home?"

"No. It's what I hope to be our home. If you want the Burner house instead, that's great too. I'm thinking we can rent this one out or something." She shook her head. "Or just let it sit. Seems a waste, but I can do what you want."

"Don't do that." He asked her what she was doing. "I don't know, but it feels like you're pressing me to do something I'm not going to do."

"What is it you think I'm making you do? See this house? If you remember correctly, you're the one that suggested we see it. I was willing to watch you sit at your dad's home and take care of you." She growled. "I don't know if you know this or not, but I find that incredibly sexy when you do that. So does my cougar."

He thought she said something like he found everything sexy, but he wasn't going to ask her to repeat it. Zach was pretty sure she'd tell him something else, and that it wouldn't be nearly as complimentary. When she started to trip up, he moved quickly, not only keeping her from falling, but helping her to one of the many chairs that seemed to have migrated from the deck into this room.

"I talked to Burt about you." He knew that. Burt had told him everything she'd asked and what he'd told her. "He told me that you have a copy of my hospital records, as well as a personal background. You could have asked me instead of snooping around behind my back."

"I never even opened the envelope that he gave me." He sat on one of the wire spools that he'd been using for a table on the deck the last few weeks. "And if he didn't make it clear, I will. I never asked for the reports on you. I don't need them to tell me anything about you. I know firsthand."

"You can't know my medical history." He nodded. "Okay, smart ass. What kind of meds are they giving me, and what do they do to me?"

"I know what they do to you, but not much else. You're on pain medication, I have no idea the name brand, but it puts you out quickly. I had to look that one up…I had no idea that drugs could affect a human so fast. But it said that you could be just the kind of person that doesn't take a lot of medications in the first place, and that might be why you're so affected." She didn't say anything as he continued. "You take a low dose of vitamins right now. I don't know what either, but you're worried that you're not eating well and take it just in case."

"You can read my mind." He nodded. "So what am I thinking right now? And if you tell me it's about sex, then I'm going to know that you're lying."

"Right now your emotions are too high for me to get clear. But I do know what you've been thinking about. You've been thinking that I'm going to be disappointed in you because of what happened to you. You want to like me but are afraid of me hurting you. I promise you right now, I won't on either of those things. And I'll never leave you. There is some fear about being able to use the stairs should you live here. The master suite is on the ground floor, so that gives you plenty of time to get better before you have to tackle those. And you are thinking about sex. With me. And if you'll be as big a letdown as you were to other men." Zach moved off the spool as he made his way to her. "When you kissed me yesterday, all I could think about later was if there was that much passion in your kiss, you might well kill me when we come together. And that the way you tasted, the way your body felt in my arms? It was wonderful. More than that, it was spectacular."

"I haven't ever been any good at sex." He told her that it was because she'd not had the right man in her life. "Are you saying that you can change that? I'm sorry, but I don't think you're right on this. I know you'd like to think you're always right, but you're not on this."

"What a shame. Perhaps I can prove it to you." He watched her face, the emotional storm that she was having. "We can smell you."

"We?" He nodded. "You mean your cat wants to have sex with me too? Oh no you don't. I will not...that's just sick."

"I agree." He wanted to laugh at her expression. "What I meant for you to know was, while he'd never want to have sex with you, he would enjoy lapping at your wet pussy until you came. Fucking you with his tongue. It's longer and thicker than mine, and rough. I'm betting that if he were to come forward right now, he'd bring you so many times, you'd be weak with it."

"No." But they both knew that her no wasn't as strong an objection as it had been before. "Besides, I'm still healing. I mean, it might be months before I can have sex with anyone, much less with you."

"I understand." He did too. Zach might not have read her file, but he really could read her mind. Thanks to Susie. "So long as you don't rule out that it could happen. We're mates, as you know, and I need you."

He and Susie had been exchanging blood, all of them had, so that if anything happened to any of them, they'd be able to find each other. Also, they'd be able to talk, each of them, on a different path, but also as a group. But when he'd bitten into Susie's tiny wrist, he'd gotten a lot more than he'd bargained for, than either of them had bargained for. Something had transferred between the two of them.

Since then, she'd been teaching him how to filter out all the thoughts of everyone and listen to a single being. It had been much harder than he'd thought it would be. But with Tisha, and here in this house alone, he could hear every single one of her doubts and thoughts.

"You're too nice, anyone ever told you that before?" He laughed and told her not recently. "Well, you are. I keep expecting you to be pissed at me. Or at the very least to give up."

"I'm not giving up on us, Tisha." He pulled her to him, not giving her any time to object to his kiss. And when he lifted his head, his heart rate was going fast as he could hear hers beating. He thought about pulling away, leaving to give her time, but he wanted to.... No, that wasn't it...he needed to prove to her that she was desirable to him. That he needed her too.

There were no beds in the house. Barely enough things finished to be calling it a home. But he knew that there were firm walls, chairs that he could use, and if all that failed, there was the deck. Zach had a moment of clarity as he realized what he was thinking.

Instead of forcing her hand, which what he was about to do, he set her down on the floor, but didn't let her go. Kissing her, giving her as much passion as he was feeling, he looked down at her.

"Right now, at this very moment, I'm having a hard time being a nice guy." She smiled at him. "If you knew what was going on in my head right now, you'd be running in the other direction."

"No. I don't think so. I'm excited about having sex with you, but it saddens me to no end to know that you're going to find me lacking." He just shook his head. "Zach, for as much as I think this is a mistake about us being mates, a major one at that, I do want you to take me. Maybe then I can have a great memory of you and me together, and you'll understand what I'm talking about when I said I'm not very good at sex."

Picking her up in his arms, he took her to the woods. If she thought that this was going to be a good memory for her, he was going to give her one she'd never forget. But as far as it being the only time with this woman, she was sadly mistaken. Tonight was going to be the beginning of something pretty amazing.

~~~

The woods were dark, thick with trees and undergrowth too. She knew that in a few weeks, less if the weather was any indication, the trees would be bare and the ground would be bright with their fallen leaves. It would be a glorious sight, one she knew she'd miss if she moved back to her home.

As soon as Zach set her down on her feet again, she looked up at him.

"Do you trust me?" She nodded. "Good. The first thing I'm going to do is beg you not to run. If you do, then this will only be fun for one of us. And it won't be me. I'd very much like for you to strip down."

"I can't run that—naked? Out here, where.... Well, what if someone came along?" He grinned at her and told her his cat would take care of them. "You mean, he'll come out and kill them?"

"No. Now, if you would be so kind as to be naked for me, then I can see that glorious body of yours." She was suddenly shy. No one but the hospital staff and her doctor had seen her since she'd been released. "Don't do that, Tisha. I'm aware that you're hurt and how badly. I want to see you. All of you."

Nodding, she pulled her sweater off. After dropping it on the ground, she paused to watch Zach take off his shirt. She wondered if he would leave the hat on, the kind that seemed to be worn by all the men in this family, and decided that she'd think of him this way, later in her memories of this night. But when he reminded her to hurry, she turned her back to finish up.

When she turned around, she held her blouse to her belly. It was healing, but not even close to being well. She also knew that she'd be scared too, very badly, but she kept telling herself that she was alive, and that was what counted. Zach was standing in just his pants, but they were opened all the way and his shoes were off. The hat, she was happy to see, was still there. He tilted it back enough that she could see his eyes. They were dark with need.

"You remember, I can read your mind." She did, and thought of all the things he might do to her. "Christ woman, you might kill me yet. Drop the shirt, baby. It's time."

"I don't know.... You're so beautiful, and I'm...well, I'm not whole." He kissed her, taking the blouse from her fingers and dropping it when he stepped back. "Don't look at me."

"I think you're the most beautiful creature I've ever

seen." She looked at him through watery eyes. "Now, don't run, remember that."

Then he was gone. The cat, a big beautiful cougar, sat down on his ass and stared at her. Tisha knew realistically that it was still Zach, but he was also sort of scary like this. Reaching out her hand to touch his head, he moved closer to her and purred.

"You're so soft. I don't know why, but I thought you'd be stiff." Zach's laughter entered her head. "Can you talk to me like this?"

I can. I didn't want to tell you that I've been stiff for days without giving you time to get used to me. The cougar in me, he loves you. Tisha rubbed him behind the ears, asking Zach if he could feel that too. *Not the same way. I know that you're touching him, that he is enjoying it, but I really don't know what you're doing.*

"I'm assuming that you've done this so I'd know not to be afraid of you. To be honest, I thought I would be. You know, you're so different than you are as a human." She moaned when the cat licked her thigh. "You should come back now."

Not yet. The cat's big head pressed her back. And when she fell, gently really, against the tree, she started to stand up when he licked her pussy. *He loves the way you smell; the way you taste.*

Tisha wasn't sure that she answered him, or that she could have if she tried. The way his tongue touched her, took her, made her feel something that she'd never felt before. Desired. Needed and sexy. When he nudged her legs wider apart, she did so willingly. And when he lapped hard at her clit, she felt her body implode, then explode with the power of her release.

Come again. Let him get his fill of you.

She screamed that she was coming again. Even as one release was winding down, another more powerful one took her to newer heights, only to drop her down again and again. And when his mouth moved up her body, to touch his amazing tongue to her wound, she let him, even going so far as to pull the gauze off that had been replaced only that morning.

When he seemed satisfied with whatever he needed to taste, he made his way back to her pussy. Her legs were weak, her body spent, but she didn't want to stop, she wanted more and more, as much as he'd give her. And when Zach asked her to lie down, to spread out his shirt and lay over it, she did so without hesitation.

The big cougar moved with her, licking the cuts that hadn't been covered...the wound to her leg, the cuts above her cast on both her legs and her hand. She wished she could have removed that for him too. Tisha wanted to feel him lick those wounds as well. And when she was down on the shirt, the cat moved between her legs and brought her twice more before Zach was there.

"I'd love nothing more than to eat you myself." He sat up on his knees, holding his cock in his hand as he looked at her. "You're so beautiful. And all mine."

"Please, I need you." He didn't move, fisting his cock as he watched her. "Zach, please, just once, I need you."

"Never just once, love. You're all ours." He asked her to say it, to tell him that she belonged to them. "I need to hear you tell me that you're my mate and that you will never leave me."

"You'll tire of me." He told her never. "I want to be your mate. I would love to know that you're going to love me forever. But I'm afraid. So very afraid, Zach."

"I won't ever let anyone hurt you again. I will love you forever." He moved over her body, not quite touching it, but

101

she could still feel his heat. "I need to hear you say it, Tisha. Tell me you're mine."

His cock was there; she could feel the thick crown of him as he moved just enough to tease her. She was ready to beg him, to tell him that she would love him forever if he took her, when it occurred to her that she did. She loved him. Tisha loved the big man and his cat.

"I love you. You belong to me, and I to you."

His cock slammed forward, not just taking her breath away but giving her something as well. He gave her life, meaning, and hope. As he fucked her, gently for a bit, then harder, she wrapped her legs around his thigh, trying her best not to beat him too badly with her cast. And when he nuzzled her neck, licking the pulse she knew was pounding there, she loved that he was going to bite her. And when he did, she'd belong to him forever.

"Bite me when you come. Just...please, bite me." She nodded, nearly cross-eyed with the need to come now. "Now, baby, now."

His teeth tore into her flesh. It wasn't as painful as she'd imagined, but wonderful, and when she pulled his throat to her mouth, he shifted in her arms so that she could take what she wanted. And Tisha found that she wanted his pulse too.

Licking the hard vein, Tisha sank her teeth into him, tearing through his corded muscle as she did so. His blood filled her mouth, the coppery taste of him and the essences of all of him leaving her wanting more. Sucking hard on the wound that she'd created, the wonderfully sweet and hot, blood filled her mouth again and again as she swallowed it down. Tisha saw stars dance around her vision as a climax like none other took her apart. Then things just snapped out.

When she woke she was covered up by a blanket, and

there was a small fire going close to her. The stones around it were keeping it from spreading, but she sat up to get more warmth as she looked around. She was alone. Zach had left her.

I didn't, love. I'm here. Just running to the door to get dinner. It would just figure you'd wake now to find me gone. I'm sorry about that. Truly I am. He laughed. *Are you hungry? I don't know about you, but I'm famished. I hope you don't mind pizza with extra meat, but I ordered it before I thought to ask you. I will next time, I promise. And I have water for you and me in the cooler near the tree.*

Wrapping the blanket he must have gotten for her around her toga style, she made her way to the tree. The cast was wet now, and she knew that she'd have to have someone look at it soon, but right now she was feeling too good. When she saw Zach coming back with three large boxes and a stack of napkins, she had a moment of worry that someone was joining them.

"No one is coming. It's just the two of us." He sat down on the rug that he'd brought too. "We worked up a hell of an appetite, and I'm hungry. I'm sure you are too."

And suddenly, she was starved. Her belly rumbled and her fingers were shaking so much for a slice that she didn't even bother with the napkins, but ate it like someone that hadn't eaten in a month. And damn, it was good too.

They had three pieces each before she felt she could speak without food in her mouth. Picking up her fourth slice as he set the now empty box aside, she felt suddenly shy. And out of sorts. So instead of taking her weird feelings out on him, she ate quietly.

"I have to work in the morning. Actually, all day. I wanted to know if you like our house, or is it going to be the Burner one?" She looked at him, wondering what he was talking about. "This one here. I know that it needs some work, but I have to show the Burner house again in the morning, and wondered which one you'd prefer to live in. I'm easy either way, so long as you're there with me."

"This is your home." He told her that it was their home. "What would you do if I said I'd rather live in the Burner home?"

"Buy it. I can borrow enough money to get it started for us. I'm pretty sure that Landon would cut me a great deal." She asked him about this one. "I don't know. As I said, perhaps we can rent it out to a foreman on one of the ranches. It's no big deal. The house, that's all it is. I want to make a home with you, where you're happy."

Happy. It wasn't a word that she was familiar with of late. It was as if all of that had been sucked out of her the moment she realized that there was someone in the house with her that day. Then Alex had nearly killed her. She looked over at the house that was still, for the most part, under construction.

It was beautiful now, and would be more so when it was complete. There really were boxes of things in his barn to use in the house, as he'd mentioned to her earlier. Shutters for all the windows. Two sliding doors for the dining room that would make it so that a person could easily move out onto the deck that was finished. She realized then that the outer things were done...the deck and roofing, as well as windows, because of the lateness of the year. He had worked hard on this, made it his home, yet was willing to give it up for her.

"I want to live here. I know that you and I are going to have a lot of working out to do. And that we're going to need a learning curve on how to be together. I've been alone for a long time. But I think, in the end, we can make this work." He laughed and she looked at him. "You think I'm being funny?"

"No. I think you're being you. And I love it, and you. I love you, Tisha, with everything I am. And I know that we can make this work. We're mates." He pulled her to him then and kissed her. "You and I are going to have a great deal of fun making that house over there a home."

She hoped so. And if she was honest with herself, she was excited about it too. She was happy, she realized in that moment. Very happy.

CHAPTER 8

Alex was taking a shower when she heard the noises downstairs. She knew that she'd locked up, making sure that no one bothered her as she did the Lord's work. As she turned off the water, careful not to knock anything over, she took out a towel and began drying off, keeping her weapons of sainthood near her.

She'd begun to think of herself as a saint just the day before. Her work was being shown all over the world now, and people were certainly talking about her. Alex thought they had her message all wrong, however, saying that she was only out for murder. But she and her Lord knew the true nature of her work for him, and he'd keep her safe. She was working for a greater cause, and she was happily cleaning up the whores that dared to invade the schools where little minds could be persuaded to do the same thing, follow in their footsteps.

"Hello?" Alex picked up the gun that she'd gotten from another whore's house when she heard the man's voice. The gun was smaller, so it fit her hand better. "Is anyone here? Jamie?"

Jamie had gone to her maker, she wanted to tell the man. Alex had dispatched her not an hour ago. Wrapping the towel around her, knowing that she was going to have to end this poor man's life now that he'd invaded her area, she moved into the hallway just as she heard him crying out.

"Oh my God. Oh my God, Jamie!" The footsteps were fast as he moved around. Alex knew what he'd found...the whore hadn't gone as easily as the others had, and Alex had lost her temper.

Jamie had questioned her faith. Asked her why she thought her Lord would have her do such a horrific thing. How dare her claim that Alex was out for her own good. Jamie had called her a murderer and a monster. A monster was something that killed for no cause. Alex had a good reason for what she was doing. Her Lord had told her to. Then Jamie had laughed at her, even as she was hitting her with her blessed hammer.

And then, like before, Alex had blanked out. When she woke, standing there naked and covered from head to toe in blood, she had been surprised that the thing in front of her had once been a person. And that her hammer, one that she'd had her Lord bless for her, was broken in two pieces.

The man came out into the hall where she was then. He was covered in blood; his shirt and tie were marred with more than just blood, she knew. As he stood there staring at her, his phone to his ear, she moved toward him, lifting the gun even as she took her first step.

The pain in her right arm jerked her back, and that was when she noticed that he had a weapon too. That wasn't right. There were no guns used against her as she did her Lord's work. She fired at him as a second, then a third shot hit her, once in the arm, the last one in the leg as the man fell. The phone still at his ear, she heard him screaming that an intruder was in his house, someone had murdered his wife.

And that he was looking at the woman from the news. Her, he was talking about her.

Alex was hurting, but not too badly. She was also covered in blood again, but her own this time. When he fired at her again, this time splintering the wood just to the left of her face, she backed away from him. This man was insane...he was shooting at the right hand saint of her lord. Turning away, she grabbed her bag and moved down the stairs.

You must kill him. Go back and take care of him. He is here in the den of the whore. Alex was ready to do just that when another shot was fired just below her feet. And thankfully, her Lord saw the need for her to get out and to safety. *Leave, leave here before he kills you, my child.*

She was out the door in seconds, the man still chasing her, screaming at her to stop. But she had a mission, a duty to her Lord, and he had told her to leave. Running for cover, keeping the towel in place and her weapon out, she dodged behind trees and cars until she no longer heard the man.

Alex would have to go back, she knew. Her mission was to end the world of whores and their familiars, just what that man was, and she wasn't going to fail again. Alex knew that for every one that she dispatched for her Lord, two more would take their place. It was a never-ending cycle, she thought.

As she made her way to the large van that she'd taken a few days ago, Alex began to feel lightheaded, her body hurting. Getting in, she closed her eyes and asked for help. If she was caught now, she told her Lord, then it would all be over. As she moved to the cargo area and lay down with her eyes closed, she begged for help and felt herself float away.

You're doing well, my child. The light was blinding; she couldn't make out what her Lord looked like, but she thought perhaps it was better this way. *When you have healed, I will give you the next list of whores. But you must go back and finish the first job. She is out there, this Tisha whore, and you must take her out before any more. It is your duty to me to make sure that the world is rid of a charlatan like her.*

"I don't know where she is. I can remember that her father lives in Ohio. Maybe that's where she's gone." He said that he'd find Tisha for her. "I hurt, my Lord. I don't wish to sound greedy or ungrateful for being chosen to help, but do you think it's possible that you could help me out?"

I help you every day, my child. She wanted to ask how, but decided it was enough that he said he did. *Go rest. The hour grows late and that man will need to be taken care of soon. You must go now before the police arrive. You rest, my child, and then move yourself to someplace safe. I wish for you to find her father after you are finished here.*

"Her father is where she'd go, I'm betting. He was forever trying to buy our friendship for his daughter. No one ever liked Tisha. I saw right through her whoring ways from the start. But I was nice and never mentioned it until you came to me." Alex had a harder time holding onto thoughts now. She'd remember something, a small bit of a memory, but it would be twisted up before she could latch onto it. Alex wondered how she was going to get Ohio, and then she remembered she had this van and the cash that she'd taken from the whores. "I will do as you command, my Lord. For it is only you that I serve."

She had no idea how long she lay there. Her body was hurting everywhere; her head was pounding like a jackhammer was in it. Sitting up, she looked around and began to take stock of her things.

Alex had plenty of clothing, all hers, that she'd put in a storage locker the morning she'd gone to the whore Tisha's house. Drinks too. Water was something that she detested unless there was nothing else, and lately, it was all she'd had. She had no food in here, which she supposed was a good thing as she had no way of keeping it cold or heating it. Now with this vehicle, she could keep her things nicer and have a bed to sleep in, even if it was just a blow up mattress.

Alex reached for the first aid kit she'd found in one of the other houses. It was thick and heavy, and she'd nearly left it behind. But now she was glad for it. Taking out the gauze, she tried to see if she was going to have to remove any bullets before wrapping the wounds up with tape, and found nothing.

"The nerve of that man. Trying to hurt me for doing your work." The Lord told her there were terrible people everywhere. "Yes, I'm beginning to see that. Thank you for showing me the way."

After she finished putting the tape on the gauze, she had to lie down again. Her head was pounding harder now, and she just needed a moment. Going to the large bag of medicines that she'd been collecting, she found a bottle that said take for pain, and took one of them. Laying down again, she tried not to think about anything but the Lord's work.

Alex didn't question the Lord for his choosing her for this work anymore. She enjoyed it…he knew that she liked it more than she should have. Work was hard…for her this was fun. To kill these monsters—because she'd figured out that was what they were—made her feel not just special, but also like she was finally finding something that she was good at. And something that gave her meaning. Alex would be canonized when this was finished, and she was sad that her parents would never see that she amounted to something other than a glorified babysitter.

Her father had never been very supportive of her. It had irritated her that he was never without his Bible, spouting his version of what it said, the meaning of each passage. To her, and the rest of the church they'd gone to when she'd been at home, he'd been a joke. Her father was no better than the sinners that never came to the blessed church at all. He was a hypocrite, plain and simple. But now, all these years later, she could see that some of his words had meaning to her.

Like he told everyone that would listen, that the world was ruled by a dick. Not just any dick either, but the government one. She'd not had any idea as a ten-year-old what that meant, and now that she was educated as well as chosen by her Lord, she still had no idea. Women, Alex had come to discover, were going to be the downfall of everything that she held holy. They manipulated men to do what they wanted, even at the risk of being just as bad as them.

"Do you suppose, when I kill off whore Tisha, that I can go somewhere and be taken care of? Not because I deserve it. But I'd like to be rested for just a time, and it would give me more energy to deal with whatever plans you have for me." The Lord said nothing. "I'm not asking for special treatment, no, not that. Just a place I can rest and recuperate. I'd be a better instrument for your works then."

There is much work to be done, my child. She loved when he called her that. Like she really was his child. *When you have finished fixing the mistakes that you have made, I will let you have plenty of rest. But first, you must rid the world of the whores of the earth.*

Alex cried then. To have her Lord point out that she'd failed him, not once but three times now, she hurt for it. Her efforts to take out the whores at the school had failed. Ridding the world of whore Tisha hadn't gone well. And now she had been told to end the man's life that had harmed her, and that had been a failure as well. She had to make up for it. Starting now.

Getting out of the van, she realized how dark it had gotten. She had no idea what time she'd left the house earlier, or for that matter, if it was the same day, now that she thought about it. Sneaking around the houses, headed back to the whore's house, Alex could see that someone was home, and that every light in the house was on. Making her way in the house as she had before, she found herself in the kitchen with a cop. He stared at her for a full minute before he lunged at her.

Taking him out was easier than she thought it would have been. After slamming the knife that she had in her hand into his chest, he stared at her, his eyes wide in shock as he died. When he got too heavy, his eyes finally closed, she laid him on the floor and took his weapon. Then before leaving the kitchen, she took his extra magazines as well as his hand radio. She had no idea if she needed it or not, but thought it might be entertaining.

Moving through the house easily, Alex saw the man sitting on the couch with a woman. Another whore, she thought. Pulling up the gun she'd taken from the cop, Alex fired twice, killing them both quickly. Before she turned to leave the room, however, she saw her face on the television.

It took her a few seconds to find the remote to turn the volume up, and she was afraid that she'd miss what they might be saying about her. They were using her school ID to talk about her. Alex had hated that picture of her, and was mad that they didn't have a better one. The Lord reminded her that it mattered little, but she was still a little peeved that they'd not asked her before using it. Then she found the remote and turned the television high enough to hear it.

"Alexandra Grace is considered armed and dangerous. The police are saying if you see her, not to approach but to call nine-one-one immediately. Again, we'll show the video that was taken earlier today by William West, husband to Jamie West, who was slain early yesterday morning." The video started then. It was her, standing there with a towel wrapped around her. And there was a bright halo of light around her head. "As you can see from the video, she's armed. Mr. West said that when she shot at him, missing him twice, he noticed that she had a knife and other weapons with her when she fled the scene of the crime. Sadly, Mrs. West, a teacher at Winton Elementary, was pronounced dead at the scene. There is—"

Alex muted the program...she didn't want to hear about what Jamie had done. They'd all be lies anyway. Only Alex and her Lord knew the truth. The video had been paused, but now it moved forward again.

When she saw herself lifting her gun to fire at the person in front of her, she was again struck by how beautiful the light was. And as the gun fired, she saw herself being hit. After that, the man recording her never had a good camera view of her. It seemed to her that he was purposefully trying to make her look bad and out of focus. Then the whore's husband was there, and she turned the sound back on.

"I had been away on a trip and wanted to surprise Jamie by getting in early. The house...I went up to our bedroom to see my wife, when...." He broke down then, sobbing loudly as the camera was on him. Then when it broke away and came back, he seemed to be in a better frame of mind. "That woman, that monster, was there, taking a shower like she'd moved into our home. While my poor wife, my lovely Jamie, who had done nothing wrong to anyone, lay in her own blood.

And all because of that monster."

"I'm not a monster. You have to believe me when I tell you, I'm not a monster. I'm doing my Lord's work. He said that she was a whore and it was my duty to go and dispatch her from this world." Alex wanted to cry…there were so many people against her right now, and it wasn't right. She slapped the man in front of her, telling him again she was working for the greater cause. "I'm not a monster. I'm doing the work of my Lord."

Gathering what she could find in the house, she was disappointed to find that the things she'd left behind were gone. Her gun that she'd dropped on the way out wasn't where she thought it was. Her clothing was missing from the bathroom, and even when she checked the laundry area, she didn't see where anyone had washed it for her. Going to the kitchen, Alex was careful not to slip in the blood that the officer had spilled, and fixed herself a meal. It was the first hot dinner she'd had in some time.

The Lord spoke to her then. *You have done well, my child.* She smiled at the warmth his praise gave her. *Now, when you have completed the other assignment, you and I will take a long rest. You have made great progress in doing my work.*

"Thank you, my Lord. I am here only to serve you."

After saying grace and then eating her meal of eggs and bacon, Alex turned on the television in the kitchen to see if anyone was praising her on it.

~~~

Harlan sat in the lobby of the hotel and observed the people. He'd been a people watcher since he'd been young, and he was sure it was what had gotten him into police work. When a very tall man came into the area and headed to the desk, Harlan kept an eye on him.

"Mr. James." He looked at the man who suddenly appeared in front of him. "I'm Zach Douglas. You don't know me, but I'm sort of here to run point for Tisha. I'm sorry, but after yesterday, you can understand our concern about just anyone showing up here."

"Yes, I understand completely." Harlan pulled out his badge, and while the young man looked it over, he looked at the man at the desk again. There was something off about him, and he wasn't really sure what it was just yet. He turned back to the Zach while still keeping an eye on the man. "Will I be able to speak to Miss Porter soon?"

"He's harmless." Harlan looked at the younger man. "His name is Will. The man at the desk. He's as harmless as a kitten. And while I can understand you thinking otherwise, trust me when I tell you, his only thought right now is to talk to his sister. The woman at the desk with him."

"Did you know that he's armed?" Zach nodded and explained. "I see. So the town knows that he's only carrying a plastic gun and is all right with that. I'm guessing that as a town, you keep an eye on him too."

"Of course. Would you feel better meeting him?" Would he? Harlan wasn't sure, but before he could tell that to Zach, he called Will over. "Will, this is Harlan James. He's an officer from where Tisha is from. I was telling him that you're helping me out."

"I have to be on alert for people I don't know. Everybody knows me, so I don't have to worry about them." Harlan nodded and took the hand that was extended in friendship. "My friends are all the Douglas boys. That's what my mom calls them, boys. They're bigger than the boys at the school ground, but they're real nice to me."

"Will is the crossing guard at the local elementary school.

He earns his keep by making sure that the kids don't get hurt there." Will smiled at Zach, and Harlan could feel the warmth of friendship from it. "Will, would you mind showing Mr. James your gun please? And remember what I told you."

"Only take it out when I know that I'm with friends. Yes, I remember, Zach." He carefully pulled out the toy gun. And when he handed it to him, Harlan was impressed that someone had taken the time to show him how to hand any weapon to another person. Butt first. "Zach and his brothers, they been letting me work for them too. I get to help pick out the colors at the new home, Child Like. You should see the playroom I helped with."

Handing him back his weapon, Harlan asked him what Child Like was. Zach looked a little uncomfortable with it, so when Will didn't answer him but simply wandered away, he dropped it for now.

"I've contacted my brother, Logan. He's bringing Tisha and her dad by now. I can't let anything happen to her." He heard laughter, a sound that reminded him of bells and harps, and turned to the doorway again. The vision there, the woman looking up at the two men with her, had his heart beating faster. Christ, she was a beauty. Zach spoke to him then, his voice low and full of humor. "I can smell that you're human, Harlan, but you've been around shifters, am I correct?"

"Human? I...yes, I am. And I do know...you're not human, are you?" Zach shook his head, his eyes never leaving the woman. "You know her?"

Zach laughed and turned to him. "You do as well. It's Tisha." Harlan looked back at the woman and watched her face as she got closer. Christ, it was her. "She's happy, and she's my mate. So if you know anything of our kind, you'll live a good deal longer if you don't touch her. I don't want to have to kill you on your first day here."

Harlan didn't want that to happen either. And he was pretty sure that young Zach wasn't kidding about killing him. There was a look in his eyes, one that said he could be friendly and kind, but don't ever touch what he considered his.

This Tisha Porter was nothing like the poor woman that he'd seen in the hospital a few weeks ago. She glowed with good health and happiness. And he'd bet anything it had to do with Zach Douglas.

"Hello, Mr. James." He nodded and she sat down. "While I'm feeling much better, everyone insists that I rest when I can."

"As you should. Listen to the experts and family, Miss Porter, and you'll heal a good deal faster." And he could see that was the case too. While she was still using a cane to get around, she didn't look beaten any more. There had been cuts, deep and long, on her cheek and neck that looked healed. Not only that, but there didn't seem to be any scarring. "You look amazing."

The laughter again. Harlan felt out of his element, not like he was the butt of a joke, but simply out classed or something. And he also knew, from his friends that were shifters, that whoever these people were, they could protect her better than he could.

"I have some news and some questions. I'm sure you've seen it on the news the last couple of days, but we have confirmed that it was Alex that has been killing the other teachers. And the information that I was sent that you remembered helps me a great deal. I just have a few questions for you." Zach sat on one side of her, taking her hand, and her father sat on the other.

There was tension there, not a lot, but enough to have

Harlan feel like Randall either didn't approve of his daughter being watched by young Zach, or he was worried about Alex. When he turned to her to ask her about the names that Alex had called her, Harlan saw that the two younger people were in love. He wondered then if this was a match that Randall didn't approve of. But he had business to attend to, and speculating about men and their daughters wasn't getting it done.

"She called me a whore. Several times, as a matter of fact." Harlan nodded and looked at his notes as Tisha continued. "She said that she had to kill me, that I'd been sleeping around...no wait, she said that I'd been selling myself for long enough. I'm not sure where she might have gotten that idea from, but her next words scared me more than you can imagine. She said that she was there to do the Lord's work, and that she was to get rid of my kind."

"I'm sorry, what?" He waited for her to repeat what had been said to her. "She said that the Lord had instructed her to kill you?"

"Yes. Is that important?" Harlan leaned back on the couch and thought about this. "Mr. James?"

"In my line of work, you run into all kinds of people. Most of them are just out to even a score. Sometimes it's an accident, but then there are the ones, like Alex, that think that some higher power is telling them that they should murder. Of all the kinds of killers that I've had to deal with, those to me are the scariest." Zach asked him why. "They believe that they're on a mission. Have a duty, I guess you could call it, to finish whatever they've started."

"You mean she's going to try and come after Tisha." Harlan nodded when Zach spoke again. "She won't. I mean, she can come here and try, but she won't hurt her. Not again."

"I'm not saying that you can't stop her, but let me make something clear to you from the start. I want you to be as prepared as you can be. When she comes here, because now I have no doubt that she will, she will let nothing stop her. No locked doors will stop her, no men around Tisha will deter her, nor will she have any issues in killing anyone that is with Tisha." Zach nodded, but Harlan wasn't so sure he understood. "If you're with her, in the same house, same yard, she will kill anyone and everyone that is there. It will be her mission. You understand that, don't you?"

"Yes. But there is something that you might not understand about us. My family, we're not your run of the mill people. We're cougars. All of us." Harlan nodded, but before he could say that they could be killed as well, Zach continued. "The man standing at the door is a bear. The gentleman near the desk is a vampire. The two people that cleaned your room today, one is a wolf, the other a tiger. They're all here…their sole purpose was either to kill you or tell us that it was safe to come here. And trust me when I tell you, no one would have ever found your body."

"She has a gun. And has killed a cop. A lot of men and women will be disappointed if they can't see her brought to justice." Zach said nothing. Harlan looked around the room. "What if I told you, just between us, that I hope to fuck she comes here and you can give her your own kind of justice? That I think that even with her guns and her Lord on her side, you can take her down, and I hope for it."

"Oh, have no doubt about that, Harlan, she will go down." Harlan nodded and stood. "When are you leaving?"

"I don't think I'm going to. Not just yet anyway." He looked over at Randall, who had not said a word. "Do you think that he can do this? Protect your daughter so that nothing happens to her?"

"I do. I don't like that he is better equipped to do it than I can, even with all my money, but I'm sure he can. Someone showed me...." Randall looked at the man at the door, then the vampire at the desk. "Let's just say that I've seen the light myself, and know they can keep her safe where I can't."

Harlan wondered about that. He didn't ask, but he thought it was funny. Whoever had shown Randall the light, they must have been very persuasive or had some big balls. Whatever it was, Harlan didn't want to go up against them in a negative way.

CHAPTER 9

The paperwork wasn't complete. Emma compared what she had found out while out on leave to what Beth had given her. Instead of giving her all the information that she'd asked for, she had about one third of it. And even that was full of holes and missing vital information. She looked for the playground contract and found it missing, along with the gates that were to be replaced at the school bus lot, the painting of the fire hydrants, and the new stop signs at two intersections that she'd earmarked for emergency funding. None of them were on the list that Beth had given her.

"Beth?" Emma heard her cursing—now that she was a cat, Emma could hear all sorts of things she'd not been able to before—and frowned. Beth had been...well, she'd been distracted today, sort of sad looking. "Beth, can you come in here please? I'd like to go over the file you gave me."

"Just a minute." Emma wanted to get up and go to her, find out what was wrong. Glancing down at the file in front of her, she had a feeling that she might know some of it. Beth was talking to her father-in-law again, Emma knew. The lines had been tapped last week, along with some cameras being positioned outside her apartment door to see the comings and goings of those who came to see her. The father-in-law, Joe

Rogan, spent more time at his son's house than his son did. "I'm on the phone. I'll be there in a minute."

Yes, Emma thought, there was something very wrong with her. There was a heavy tone to her voice. Her words were, while sharp, sad too. When Beth finally came into her office, Emma showed her the list she'd handed her, hoping that making her mad might bring her out of her funk.

"I think there is some work missing." Beth took the file and flipped through it, then handed it back as she sat down. "Where is the work on the hydrants?"

"Hydrants? I thought the Boy Scouts were doing those. I'm pretty sure they were. And honestly, why do you even care?" Emma ignored the question and asked her why the city had paid Rogan Construction for the work. "Oh, I don't know then. Maybe he bought up all the material and then provided it to them for some kind of badge. They're forever getting badges for stuff like that."

"Well, can you tell me if there is a merit badge for building the playground in the park? Or perhaps there is one for the stop signs being put up at Miller and Main?" Emma laughed a little, but her heart wasn't in it today. For some reason, the thought of making this girl admit what she was doing with her father-in-law no longer had any appeal. "What's the matter, Beth? Is there anything I can do for you? Or help you with?"

"Isn't there something else you could be working on?" Emma was shocked by not just the question, but her tone too. "Look, I'm working really hard here, and you're giving me jobs that are frankly beneath me. If you want to see about jobs, you should go over to the new building construction that is going on over at the hotel that is being renovated. Their permits aren't up to date, and they're not using the city contractors to do the work either."

"You mean your family contractors." Beth said nothing. "There is no reason for that building to use city workers, if we had any, because it's privately owned and operated. And as of yesterday, because I checked, all their permits are up to date, and have been, and work has resumed."

"No. You can't do that." Emma asked her why not. "You just.... Look. Maybe you don't understand how this is supposed to work. They come here, apply for a permit to build or whatever. Then I send out one of the guys who works for Rogan to see about how much the building is going to impact the city. Most of the time it's taken over by the city to do, and that's when bids are put in to do it. It's really cut and dry. I take care of that, as I take care of everything, it feels like."

"But Rogan's are not city workers, nor do they have a contract with the city for a permanent license to do work. In fact, I don't think I've ever seen them apply for a permit to work anywhere in this city." Beth told her it was implied. "By who? Not me. And so you know, as of an hour ago, Rogan Construction is being audited."

"What the fuck? Are you trying to ruin my family business?" Emma just stared at her when Beth started pacing. "You're not playing by the rules, Emma. I don't know where you got it in your head that you can just come in here and change things after they've been set up, but you need to just back off."

"I'm the mayor, Beth, perhaps it's you that needs to back off."

Beth just paced, and while she was doing that, Emma reached out to Mason, who was with the police on the floor below them. *You watching this?*

Yes, I am. Uppity little thing, isn't she? Oh, and the Feds have already gone into the offices of Rogan and taken the computers and all paperwork they can find. And I think they're at the house now. For sure they've gone to Beth's. Did you know that when she was hired she signed a contract that said whenever they needed them, she was to willingly turn over her computers, both personal and business? Emma said that she'd turned it in yesterday when she'd found it. *See? Right from the very beginning, I knew you'd make a better mayor than me. But let me ask you something...do you think she'd be so willing now?*

No. I really don't. Hang on. Beth turned to her and started to cry. *Oh no, I knew something was wrong. Perhaps it would be a good time for someone to come in here too.*

"He told me that you had to go. I thought that it was a wonderful idea, then I realized that I have no idea how to go about getting you dead." Emma asked her what plan she'd come up with. "Kill you. I mean, that was my plan. But I just couldn't figure out a way to make it happen and not get caught. Then I realized that that woman, Tisha, is in town, and that she was hanging with your family. You'd not believe how many thoughts of taking you out I had in my head. Then...then I had to go to the doctor."

Emma just watched her, knowing that as a cat there would be no way for Beth to attack her and come out on top. But when she pulled out a gun and laid it in her lap, Emma asked Mason again to send someone in.

We're working on it, honey. There is something wrong with the elevators. I'm taking the stairs up now. She told him to hurry. *Are you in danger, love? Is she trying to hurt you?*

No. I'm not sure, but I don't think she has any intentions of harming me. There is something very off about her today. He said he was nearly there. *Just be careful. I don't know what is up her sleeve, but I don't want either of you hurt.*

"Tell me, Beth. You should know that with all that is

going on with you and your father-in-law, people are aware of it. You're going to go to jail." Beth nodded, but didn't look at her. Her entire focus was on the gun in her lap. "Beth, look at me."

"I was going to have a baby. I was so excited that I got up every morning and put my hand on my belly to feel it. I know that it was much too early, but I needed the connection." Emma said nothing to Beth, but told Mason to wait. "Then my husband found out. Joe knew, of course. But Joey and I, we never talked about having children. So when I told him I might be pregnant, he hit me. Just backhanded me hard enough to knock me against the wall of our bedroom."

"He found out about you and his dad, didn't he?" Beth just nodded. "What happened then? Did he go after his dad?"

"No. He didn't blame him at all. Said that I was a fucking cunt. His own wife, he called me a fucking cunt. Then he picked me up from the floor and tossed me across the room." Beth looked at her then. "He told me that he was filing for divorce. And that he was going to tell his mom too, so that she'd divorce his father. Do you know what happened then?"

"You lost the baby." It was in the report that had been given to her yesterday. Beth had shown up at the hospital a few days ago with a miscarriage. "I'm so sorry, Beth. No matter who the father was, he had no right to do that to you."

"It's too late now. Not just for the baby, but me as well." Beth picked up the gun, but with the muzzle in her hand. Emma felt safe in thinking that she was going to turn the gun over to her. "There is a file on my computer of all the accounts that you need to examine with the Rogan name on it. Some of them are overseas, and a few of them are in other states. We used a lot of the cash that was paid out for jobs that weren't done, but I started squirreling it away so that when it was time, Joe and I could run off. I don't think that's going to happen. So I'm all alone. So very alone."

"I'm sorry, Beth. But you have to know that you're both going to jail. Not only did you steal funds, but you committed fraud as well. There is no hope for either of you." Beth nodded, but said nothing. "Is there anyone that I can call for you? Do you need an attorney?"

"I honestly don't have any idea. And even if you were to call one for me, I can't afford it. I'm pretty sure you have me pretty locked up, don't you? I've come to realize over the last few days that you're not nearly as horrible as I made you out to be. And for that, I'm profoundly sorry." Beth looked at her, tears in her own eyes. "How could he not want a child of his, or even a grandchild? I've seen you and your husband together. That's what I guess I thought it would be like for Joe and me when we got away."

"Not every person in the world likes children." Beth nodded. "I need you to turn over the gun, Beth. The police are here. They need to take you downtown. If you cooperate, it will go a long way to what sort of sentence you get."

"I'm so very alone, Emma. I should have been a nicer person." She didn't move, and neither did the police as they stood by the door. "I never liked you when we were children. Even as a kid you were better than me. You never rubbed it in my face, and no matter how many times I tried to outwit you, you always managed to come out on top. Why is that? You had a scumbag for a brother, and here you are mayor of the city and well thought of."

"I tried my best not to let you bother me. I let whatever you said to me, did to me, go. There was no point in holding onto my anger. It did me little good, and after I left here to go to college and work, I never thought of you again." Beth nodded again. "Beth, they need you to turn over the gun."

"Joe has the money in an account that he thinks I don't know about. There is over seven hundred thousand dollars in it. He not only scams the city, but he takes kickbacks from some of the merchants who he bullies into it." Emma started writing down names as soon as Beth said them. "His wife, Sandra, my mother-in-law, she's not as innocent as she makes out either. There is a man she's been fucking around too. And she has her own little stash. It's in the barn under the old Chevy that her husband has been *'working'* on for ten years."

Emma looked at Beth; she was so different than the woman that she'd been an hour ago. No less sad, really, but she looked more defeated, broken. Emma asked her again for the gun. When she lifted it up, Emma stood. She'd ask for leniency for what she'd done for them.

"You'll need a good attorney, but I'll talk to them on your behalf." Beth nodded. "It's over now. All the money, thanks to you, will be returned. I'm sorry it had to end this way."

"It's our fault. I should have known better than to get involved with him." She stood up too, the gun hanging from her fingers. "My baby didn't need to be murdered, you know. My own husband, he took from me too. Just like his dad did. And now, now I'm going to jail for a very long time, and for what? For a good fuck? A murdered child? I'm sorry, Emma, and thank you. You're a good person."

Before anyone could move, Beth put the gun to her temple and shot herself in the head. There hadn't been a moment of hesitation either. She just said her piece and did it. Emma felt the hot spray of her blood hit her in the face before she realized what Beth Rogan had done. She'd ended her own life.

~~~

Tisha asked the doctor to repeat himself. "I said, we can

remove this cast. The bones have healed nicely, and there won't be any trouble like you were told about stiffening muscles or pain later, I would imagine. I've also put in an order to have x-rays done of your hand and your head, just to make sure what I'm seeing is right. You're healed, Tisha. Congratulations."

"But that's not possible. You said, just last week when I came in, that I'd have to go at least another five weeks with the cast, and that the headaches would lessen over time but may be there for a while longer. You said that." He nodded and grinned. "I want a second opinion."

"Okay." He got up and left her there. The gown she had on was barely covering her, so when the door opened, she pulled it back over herself. The doctor was still grinning like a loon, but he wasn't alone this time. "This is all the second opinion you need, I think. I'll be with another patient when you're ready in here."

Tisha looked at Zach when he sat down. There was something going on here, something that she wasn't getting. And when he took her hand in his, she jerked it back and told him to explain.

"I will. But I want to hold onto your hand while I do it. If you remember, when you get...excited, you tend to pull my hair." Her face heated up to the point where she wanted to fan herself. "I'm going to explain to you what we think happened. Okay? When you bit me, taking my blood into your body, it healed you. And every time we made love—which, if you ask me isn't nearly enough—you take a little more. Because of what I am, you're healing quicker. That's the first part of what I need to tell you."

"I don't understand. And just how many parts are there?" He took her hand again and kissed the back of it. He told her three, so far. "Zach, what do you mean, your blood healed me? I really am having a difficult time hanging on here."

"Okay. Now, part two. When you and I made love the first time, you were weak. Your injuries were pretty extensive, and there was a lot of blood loss still. While you were with me, your body was still in the process of healing." She nodded and told him to go on. "When...I should start with this. When one of our kind changes a person, converts them, they bite them in the belly region, the throat, and the leg. These bites give a human a lot of pain, and our saliva hits the system quickly to heal those areas. Understand?"

"You're saying this because you want to convert me." He nodded, then shook his head. "Perhaps you should continue. Right now, I want to scream at you for not getting to the point."

"Yes. The point. You were already hurt. My bite and my cat's saliva from eating you hit your already injured system hard. Like you were being converted." She just stared at him, trying her best to keep up. "The combination of the two things, the injuries and us having sex, did it."

"Did it? You mean, it healed me but did more than that." Zach smiled and nodded. "So what you're saying to me, and I hope that I'm right, is that I might be a cat too."

"Would that be so bad?" That wasn't very helpful. "I've talked to Mason and my Aunt Georgie, who said that she loves you dearly by the way, and they think that it didn't hurt you as much as it might have because you were already on pain killers. Not heavy doses, but enough so that when you converted, it was for the most part painless. You're a cat, love. A cougar like me."

It took a moment for what he was saying, everything he was saying, to sink in. "Did you know that I was a cat? I mean, before this?"

"No. I mean, I think my cat knew. He's been acting sort of strange around you, even you have seen that." She had and nodded. "Anyway, I had it in my head that converting you would be painful for you, biting you while you were still hurt, and that recuperating like you were it would be too much for you, so I never brought it up. I knew that my blood would heal most of the smaller wounds, but I never thought of it converting you as well."

"So, I'm a cougar." He nodded. "I can shift and run with you in the woods if I want. That's what you're telling me. Please, tell me that's what you're saying, Zach. I could use some good news right about now."

"This is the best news, I think. But you can't shift, not yet anyway. There is the matter of the cast. I don't know what that would do to your cat should you shift with it on. It's like a great many things that could happen to your cat if you're, say, tied up when you shift. And when you're in a tight place with your human self, it could —"

She lifted her hand and he shut up. "Can you please go and get the doctor and tell him to take this cast off me? I have a need.... Does it hurt?" He shook his head. "I want to go and be a cat. Like you are."

"I understand that, but I have to tell you one more thing. Okay? The last part." She nodded and asked him if it was bad. "No. I mean, I hate to bring this up, but I have to tell you some things first. You are aware of your inability to have children, so I want to tell you that even though you're a cat now, you still can't have children. We can heal things, but not replace. Understand?"

"Yes, but damn it, get to the fucking point again. But if it's bad news, please don't tell me now." He told her it wasn't, but still didn't speak. "Zach, I've fallen in love with you. But right now, I'd gladly kill you for keeping me waiting like this. Tell me, for Christ's sake."

"Do you want a child?" He'd just told her that she couldn't have one, so she wasn't sure where he was going. "There was a baby born just this morning, his parents are both deceased. There was an accident and.... He's a cougar, and needs someone to take him before he gets in the system."

"A baby?" He nodded. "What happened? I mean, you said you just found out. Do you know them, the parents of this little boy?"

"They're a part of our pride. I know them both, not as well as Mason does, but yes.... They were traveling back home from a short vacation and were hit by a drunk driver not far from here. They tried everything to save them, but they were.... The damage was too extensive for them to be able to shift and heal. Mr. Wayne taught at the college, his wife was a nurse in the clinic here. They had to take the little boy by Caesarean section a while ago to save his life. The police had found a relative, a grandmother, and she isn't in a position to raise him." She asked him about anyone else. Other children. "No, he would have been their first. And since the accident, the police have tried to contact Mr. Wayne's mother, but she.... She won't have anything to do with the child either. Apparently, she hated the daughter-in-law and refuses the child."

"Why, was she a bad person?" He said that April was one of the nicest people that he'd met. "Well that bitch. You can tell her for me that...never mind. I'll tell her. To have a child of your own child and not want.... I'm going to keep her away from him if it's the last thing I do. When can we take him home?"

133

Zach grinned. "We have to wait until he's strong enough. While he was born healthy, even under the circumstances, he's a little weak." He kissed her on the mouth this time. "So, that's a yes? We're going to take him as our own?"

"You never doubted it, did you?" He didn't say anything. "You were afraid I'd say no? You think I'm that cruel?"

"God, no. I think you're amazing. But you've only just turned, or at least know about it, and this hasn't been the best of times lately. I wasn't sure you'd want to take on an infant too. I was hoping, but worried that you'd think it was too much." She asked him when they could see him. "Later today. I have to make arrangements with Ed, our attorney. And we have to get the house a little more...I'm having some trouble getting things finished at the house at the moment."

"Money." He didn't say anything again, and this time she took his hand into hers. "Did you know that my dad has been wanting to help you for weeks now? He said a man that can make his little girl happy and safe, he should have it all."

"I don't know your father that well. He's been around, I know that, but he's not.... I can honestly say that I never made an effort to know him when I was growing up. Not because I was afraid of him, but...well, he's sort of out of my league. Kind of like Holly and Emma were to me."

"You're a snob." He denied it, but she was having too much fun right now. "Yes, you are. A snob. My father is one of the nicest people you'll meet."

"I know that. I mean, lately he and I have been hanging out together, and I've gotten a little more comfortable around him. He's never made me feel less than him, nor has he rubbed in in my face that I can't provide for you like he has." Tisha asked him why he thought he would. "I don't know. Like I said, I'm only just getting to know him. What do you think he'll say about all this?"

"You mean the baby? Or me being a cougar?" He told her both. "I think first of all he'll be on top of the world to know that he's going to be a grandda. While he's never said anything about it, I know that he's been wanting a grandchild. As for the cougar part? I have no idea. I know that he's aware of shifters…he also knew what you were before I did. Burt, as you know, is a shifter, and introduced us into that world. I think that Dad will be happy. Oh, who am I kidding, he's going to be thrilled to death with both."

The doctor came in then and asked if she was happy with her second opinion. Laughing, she told him she was and asked to have the cast removed. After some setting up, she was put in a room where it could be done and Zach stepped out to make a few calls. One of them, she knew, was to her dad.

"I hope you don't mind, child, but I've had the nurses put together a little packet to take home with you." The doctor sat down in the chair to talk to her after he checked her leg. "It's about having a child and what to expect. Having a baby that isn't human isn't much different than most parents run into. And a lot of it will be something that you'll have to learn on your own. Like diaper changing. Feedings and so on. Like I said, much like a human child."

"I'm nervous." He told her that she should be. She was taking on a lot. "Holly and Emma, you know them. I think they'll be a great help, don't you?"

"Oh yes. Excellent source of help, there. Also, you can count on Mercedes and Georgie. You have a great family that will bend over backwards to give you anything you might need." She had a feeling there was more he wanted to say to her, and was stalling. So she started talking about nothing in general to help him.

"Zach and my dad are going to be able to get the house finished faster now. I know just which room I'd like to put the baby in. Do you know if the Waynes had a name picked out for their son?" He said he wasn't aware of any. "That's fine. We'll work his last name into his somehow so he can have that much."

"There are more." She didn't say anything because she wasn't sure what he meant. "Children that are not wanted, not planned. Just abandoned as if they were no more than a read newspaper. You have no idea how...you and Zach taking this little boy, you give me hope that there are others out there like the two of you. People willing to take on a child that no one wanted."

"How many?" He said numerous. "You know how many there are. Tell me how many children that you've run into this month."

"Ten." Her heart broke for them and for him. "Not all of them are infants. Most aren't, as a matter of fact. There is one little girl that has been in and out of the system so much that she's jaded. Not being loved, it can make a person simply give up. But this little Wayne child, you've done right by him, and that makes me think there is hope for them all."

"I'd like to see her." He shook his head and told her that wasn't what he meant. "I know, but that doesn't mean that I can't help her. Maybe not all of them, but I'd very much like to.... Zach and I can help, and we will."

By the time she was ready to go, not only did she have Loren's file, but she had a picture of her as well. Tisha knew that some way, somehow, she was going to try her best to bring the little girl home with them too.

CHAPTER 10

The trip had been exhausting. Her Lord was keeping her awake all night now, telling her what she needed to do, who had to be removed from the earth so that it would be a peaceful place, and that he was sometimes proud of her and other times disappointed. That was what had her out here now, trying to find the man that the Lord felt had slighted them. Alex had been upset as well, but had thought it not worth her having to leave her van to find him. But her Lord had been very upset when she'd dared question him about it.

You will do as you're told. Alex had dropped to the floor, her head pounding with the anger of her Lord. *He took your parking place when I wanted you to be closer to the door. There was no cause for that. You are a woman of worth, and he should have known that.*

So she got herself ready and moved out of the van. It was beginning to smell, she knew that, and so was she. But while there was money for her to take a nice hotel, the Lord had told her that people would not understand.

"Understand what?" He'd warned her about questioning him, but she felt that this time it was more of a learning thing than her wondering what she was doing. "I am only following your direction. The one that rules all."

People are not like you, my child. You are a gift to them, and I fear that they'll harm you. She had seen her picture in the paper; the news talked nonstop about how she'd murdered innocent people. *You know as well as I that had you not stepped in and taken my tasks to heart, those women would still be alive and causing harm.*

She now stood near the parking spot that the man had taken from her, while her Lord told her what she must to do him to make him realize that he'd failed the Lord. Alex hid in the shadows for nearly an hour until a car—not the one that the man had been in first, but another car—pulled into the space.

I wish for you to take him from this world by stabbing him. While you are doing my tasks, I wish for you to tell him what he has done and why you are helping him to the center of my heart. Alex paused in her step, wondering why she'd been told to bring the gun this time and not a knife. *You will need to be better prepared, my child. Next time, you will need to be ready to do my calling.*

"Yes, my Lord, I'm sorry." The man turned to look at her and she stared at him before moving. "This isn't the same guy, I don't think."

Kill him.

She leapt forward at the sound of the angry voice in her head. The gun went off three times, each of them making the man stagger back as the bullets entered his chest. When he fell back against the seat, Alex moved closer, thinking to just end him now before anyone tried to tell her she was wrong, when she felt the bullet enter her leg and throw her back.

"Police." The badge was shoved in her face, and she barely had time to read it before the man she'd shot was screaming words at her. He told her to drop her gun. She felt it being knocked away from her, and had no way of reaching for it again. The pain was incredible. "Alexandra Grace, you're under arrest for the murder...."

The man continued to speak, his words blurred from the pain, his face seeming to change to different people, people that she didn't know. When someone said her name, she opened her eyes and looked at them. She was unable to focus well, but heard the person ask her if she had any more weapons.

"My Lord said that I was to be fully armed next time." The person said something about her Lord and Alex continued. "He is a good and kind being. I have become his instrument of justice. It is my duty to rid the world of whores and their servants."

"Yeah, I just bet you have." There was a tone. And she might have said something to the person, but she felt a pinch at her arm and then things got fuzzier...her hearing was going too. "We're taking her to County General. Someone will need to ride along with us so that there is a witness that we did right by this piece of shit."

The voice of her Lord told her to get up, to show the person that she was doing his work, and that she had more work to do. But her arms were heavy, her legs wouldn't move. As she felt herself being moved, she spoke to her Lord. It was dizzying being lifted then set down hard.

Alex tried to call for her Lord before they took her away. "I need your help, my Lord. Please, I have work to do for you yet. You said that you needed me and would keep me safe. My lord?" He was quiet, for the first time in days. "Lord? Where are you?"

The Lord had left her. She had failed him again by not killing the man he'd told her to, and now her Lord was gone.

Calling out to him once more, she heard the man next to her tell her to shut up. Had she been able to, Alex might have gladly murdered him. But she didn't. Murder was a sin.

~~~

Zach moved through the halls of the hospital, trying his best to keep up with Tisha. Her dad was already there, and with him, Burt. They did not look happy. Not that he blamed them overly much…this was huge.

"She's still in surgery, and will be for another hour." Tisha took his hand in hers as her dad continued. "They said that she tried to murder an off-duty officer that had just pulled in to pick up a few things for his wife. Lucky for him, he'd been wearing his vest."

"Has she said why him? I mean, wasn't she out to kill the teachers?" Randall said he had no idea as yet, they'd only just arrived as well. Zach thanked him before telling him what he knew. "My family is looking into some things as well. Emma has a direct line to what's going on, and will let us know when she gets here."

"Good. Also, before I forget, I've called in some help with the house." Zach started to tell him no, but Tisha squeezed his hand and he didn't speak. "What with my new grandson coming home soon, I thought it would be nice if you didn't have to worry about the house and him. Besides, call it a wedding present if you want. I'm to understand there is a wedding in the works."

"We were headed downtown to get everything in order for next week. I was going to let you know when we had that worked out." Randall nodded and smiled. "You don't have to do that for the house, Randall. I'm sure that we could have gotten it done."

"I've no doubt that you would have. But like I said, my

grandson is coming home soon." They'd yet to tell anyone about Loren. But he and Tisha were sure that after the initial visit, the family would love her as much as they did.

She was a little on the defensive side. Loren was the ten-year-old that the doctor had told Tisha about. She was jaded, to the point where she was indifferent to anything and anyone. Or so she had wanted them to think. After two days of going back and forth with her case worker, Zach had called in help. Within an hour after him talking to Landon, the paperwork to see her was finished.

The first visit hadn't gone well. "So you're doing this 'cause someone fucking told you to." Loren had a mouth on her that made him slightly uncomfortable. "You don't have to do shit. I know that in a few days, some jack wad is gonna come and get me and take me back to this here fucking place."

"That's enough." He'd been about to tell Tisha that now was not the time to correct the child, but she snapped her fingers and told her to sit up in her chair, which surprisingly, Loren did. "Now, you're going to stop trying for shock value, young lady. I, for one, don't find it to be amusing or very nice. We've been trying to talk to you for the last ten minutes, and all you've done is sit there being rude and obnoxious. Either straighten yourself up, or this is not going to go well for you."

"You can't talk to me that way. I know my rights." Tisha only crossed her arms over her chest and stared her down. "You're not nice. Other people, they let me do what I want 'cause they know they're only getting paid to keep me. Well, I showed them, didn't I?"

"I'm sure you did. And now look where you are. Ten-years-old and considered unadoptable. That must make you feel like a million bucks." The girl said nothing, but Zach could tell what she was thinking...she was afraid. "And as for money to keep you, I don't need it, nor will I take it. If you come to live with us, the money that the state hands over to us will be put into an account for you to use when you've decided on a college. Zach and I have more than enough money to make you comfortable."

"You'd just give me that money? What do you want, sex? I don't like it." Zach reached into her head and found that she'd been sexually abused in two different homes since she'd been put in the system. Two places that he was going to take care of as soon as he got home. "And I don't need you telling me what to do. I got it just fine right here."

"Do you? What if I told you that coming to live with us, you'd have your own room, your own things, as well as an education? You'd have uncles and aunts, cousins, as well as grandparents." Loren looked at him and he smiled at her. Tisha continued as she sat down in the chair across from the young girl. "We have room enough for you in our home. And our hearts, if you allow us."

"They all said the same shit." Tisha only cocked a brow at her, and Loren squirmed and said she was sorry. "Look, if you don't mind, I'd just as soon stay here. I'm betting you'd have all kinds of sh...crap that you'd be making me do to have things. I'm not into child labor either."

"Suit yourself." When Tisha stood, so did he. But Tisha paused and took out a sheet of paper and wrote their names and phone numbers on it. "If you change your mind, you can call us and we'll come and talk to you. A lot of people don't think you're worth the time to try and save. But I think you're more than worth it."

That had been on Monday. As the days dragged by, they were able to get information on the couples that had abused the little girl. After Palmer and Landon found out, it was all that they could do to keep them from going to their homes themselves and taking their anger out on the four of them. As it was, they were not only in jail, but there had been several more children coming forward to talk about the abuse they'd suffered as well.

Then just this morning, he'd gotten a call from Loren. She needed him. "Can you come here? I mean, can you bring me some money? I need.... I'd like for you to come here and talk to me."

"What is it you need, Loren? I can get most anything you want, but I don't know what that is unless you tell me." He could feel her anger, not at him but at someone else. He waited to dive into her head deeper, to find the real reason she was calling, because he wanted her to tell him. "Tisha and I will have a new baby in the house we're looking forward to showing off to you. You'll be a big sister when you get here… if you want to come, that is."

"I don't know anything about babies. What will I have to do with it?" Zach told her she'd only have to love him and to be his sister. "Love it? No one loves me, so how the hell do you expect me to love it? And I know nothing about being a sister. I don't have anyone. Never did. My mom left me at the hospital when they wouldn't let her sell me off for some drugs."

He knew this. It had been in her file. What he didn't know was how she'd found out, and he knew that he would discover the truth. No one should have told her that sort of information. He told her that he would never do that.

"Why not? I'm not nice. I'm not even very good, either." He said nothing, sensing a trap. "Just this morning I took all the cereal in the place and trashed it. Wanna know why?"

He looked. For some reason, and it turned out he was

right, he didn't think she'd make other children suffer for no reason. Beneath it all, Zach thought she was a good girl.

"Because it had bugs in it and you didn't want them to serve it up to the other children in the home." She was quiet then. "I think that's one of the best things I've heard all day, Loren. Thank you for thinking of the others."

"They're kicking me out." He knew that as well. It was front and center in her mind. And that Loren was terrified. "What will I do if you don't take me? Where will I go?"

"We're coming now. All right? You just sit tight and we'll be there in twenty minutes." She cried then, and it broke his heart. "I'm coming for you, sweetheart. I'm coming now, and Tisha will be there soon too."

He had just left the tractor in the field, having only come in the house for a few more bottles of water, and caught the call. As he stood there, trying to figure out what to do, Mason came in with the news of Alex being caught. He told Mason what was going on.

"Go to your daughter, Zach. I'll take care of things here." He nodded, still not sure what he was supposed to do. "Go. I swear to you, things will be just fine. She needs you now, not when you've tried to get things done here first."

He'd gone to see her. As she sat across from him, her anger back in place, he started to ask her what had happened when she glanced at the woman that was in the room with them. He had a feeling that she was the cause of a great deal of the child's problems. Zach turned to the warden, a name that Tisha had given her that first day, and asked to be alone with the child.

"No." No other explanation, just a simple no. Standing up, she put her hand on her hip, as if she were looking for a weapon. "She's a bad one and will tell you anything. Lies, that's all she knows is lies."

"Be that as it may, I want you to get out of here, now." The compulsion hurt her, he knew it. Zach hadn't ever had an occasion to use it on anyone before, and was glad when she turned and left them. He sat back down and had to let out several long breaths before he felt like he could speak in a reasonable tone. "She's not going to bother you again."

"I didn't lie about the cereal. I can't show you it now, but I didn't lie." He said he believed her. "You do, too. How come? You got no reason to want me. That other woman, Tisha, she said you don't need the money. Why are you coming here like this? Making noises about taking me home with you?"

"Because as soon as my attorney is done with the paperwork, which is going to be moving along faster now, you are coming to our home, today if I can swing it. You will be a part of our family, and we'll take care of you. If you want that." She didn't so much as blink at him. "You said they were kicking you out. Because of the cereal incident. I don't believe that is all…what else happened?"

She looked away, then back at him before standing up and turning her back to him. When she lifted her shirt up, he wanted to find the warden and kill her. As soon as Loren sat back down, she began speaking in such a calm voice that it scared him.

"I can't be here no more, Mr. Zach. If she hits me again, and she will, I will hurt her. I'm little, but I know things that can protect me. And she might kill me, but I'm going to mess her up bad before she does." Zach reached into her mind; he didn't rape it, but he saw much more than he'd ever thought he'd see in a child's mind. Instead of telling her that things would be better, he'd make sure they were. Starting today.

He pulled out his phone. "Ed, this is Zach. I need for you

to contact Tisha and ask her to meet me at the hospital instead of the children's home. Loren has been beaten." Ed said that he'd call an ambulance. "I don't think that's necessary. Just, she can't stay here."

"Need the ambulance, son. To prove you didn't just take her out and hurt her yourself." He could see that, and thanked him for thinking of it. "I'll meet you at the hospital, and from there, I'll take over. You should know that I'm with Palmer now, and he's about to bust he's so pissed off."

"So am I. The woman here, she beat her for trying to save the other children from eating rotten food." Zach felt Loren take his hand and curl hers around his much larger one. "Ed, she's afraid and hurt. You'll make sure that she's safe for us, won't you?"

"You got that right, boy. I'm leaving now." He could just see the man wiping at his brow. "Mary just called in the troops, so you just sit tight until the police and ambulance get themselves there."

In ten minutes he was still holding her hand and letting the police talk to her. She was examined and put in the ambulance just as Ed pulled up. Instead of getting to ride with her to the hospital, Zach let the police do it. He had to fill out the paperwork to take care that nothing happened to the little girl, his little girl, again. As soon as she was settled he told her what was going on, and that Ed would not leave her until he returned. Now they were dealing with the fallout from Alex. And hopefully this would be the end of it.

"Dad, we have something to tell you." Zach let Tisha tell them about Loren while he went to the desk to ask after the woman. He didn't want Alex trying to escape, nor did he want her to die. He was afraid for his family, but he wanted answers, and if she was dead, they'd never get them.

"Mr. Douglas, there's a call for you." He took the receiver from the nurse when he said he'd take it. "I think it's another police officer. He said his name was Harlan."

"Hello?"

Harlan was talking to someone else when he answered the phone. Zach just waited. Whoever was getting the dressing down from the man had really screwed up, and Harlan was making it clear that it had better never happen again. When he came on the line again, Zach laughed.

"I hate this part of my job." Zach told him he'd not be able to do what he did either. "I called to confirm that Alex has been arrested. I heard it, but can't get any answers from anyone. And Emma, she's not in her office either. Can you help a man out?"

"She's in surgery now. Alex, not Emma. Emma had something happen at her office earlier this week, and they're dealing with that. Her office is a crime scene right now too." He asked about the woman who had killed herself and if that was her. "Yes, it was her. She had a diary on her computer that showed the mental stress she was in after losing her child. I guess she wasn't dealing with it very well, and getting caught was too much for her."

"That's just sad. People can murder and do all sorts of things that they shouldn't be doing, and something like that happens and it brings home that at one time they were human. What can you tell me about the officer that took Alex down? By the way, I'm on my way in now. I didn't come before because of the press. They don't need any more than we can give them." He told him what he knew about the cop. "Good. I'm glad to hear that it was only a couple of ribs and not him being hurt worse. The people back home, they're still cleaning up her mess. Found a couple more...never mind.

Let's just say this is one overworked cop here that's glad that she was found before she killed again."

"I'm going to have someone meet you in the lobby to bring you up, all right?" He said that would be great. "The locals have the floor pretty much blocked off. The press, as you mentioned, is out in force today. Too much going on in such a small amount of time." He told Harlan to call when he got there.

He saw his family coming toward him when he turned to see where Tisha was. Mason contacted him to tell him that he was in the emergency room with Loren. Ed had some papers to file and would return. Mason said he'd stay with Loren until she was released. Zach decided to go down and see her soon, just to make sure she was holding up well.

After checking on Tisha and making sure that she was all right, Randall told them to go and see to his granddaughter. The man looked ready to bust, he was so happy. After hugging him about half a dozen times, they made their way to the elevator. Zach realized then that he was going to be a father to two children. And he loved it.

"She's upset with us." He asked Tisha how she knew. "I asked the nurses to keep an eye on her for us. Mason isn't doing as well as you'd think. The man of a large pride is having issues with one pintsized little girl."

"He volunteered to keep an eye on her. I think he thought he could get through to her faster than we could. I'm kind of glad that he couldn't. Calming a ten-year-old would be hard on him. Mason isn't the most patient of men when it comes to not having things go his way. But he will have to get used to her, just like we will." Tisha said she wanted to take her home now. "We'll try, but Ed said they might want to keep her overnight to make sure she's going to be all right. They don't take child abuse very well around here."

"Good."

Almost the moment they entered the room, Loren started sobbing, holding their hands and thanking them. Mason slipped out of the room and Zach sat down. Tisha was climbing in the bed with Loren to hold her, and Zach felt wonderful. He had a son and a daughter now. It made all the other shit going on in his life seem a little less overwhelming.

CHAPTER 11

Harlan sat very still. He wanted to get up and hit the woman in the bed across from him, but he was pretty sure that the other police, the locals, were only tolerating him because of the big man in the corner.

Ed Clark wasn't a large man, but he certainly carried himself like he was nine feet tall with the heart of a stone cold lawyer. He simply exuded calmness and strength, and a bit of *don't fuck with me* that he could tell these men didn't get or respect. He was the kind of man that kept heads cool and tempers under control. Also, he was pretty sure that Ed might have hurt one of them if they hadn't allowed him to be a part of his.

"I don't know why you're saying these things to me. I need to be released so that I might continue the Lord's work. He calls me his child." The man standing next to him snickered at Alex. "I'm not trying to be funny. He came to me and told me that they were sinners, and that I needed to bring them to justice."

"You mean murder them. And I don't believe for a minute that you have this connection with God, lady." Harlan started to stand up and tell the man to shut up when Ed cleared his throat. With a small shake of his head, Harlan sat back in his chair and waited. The cop continued to speak. "You killed nine women and four men. And you blew up a school and could have killed seven hundred other people. You're saying that the Lord had told you to do that?"

"That's enough." Ed stepped forward and looked at him. "Would you please take over this case for the city, Harlan? This man is being relieved of his duties."

"What do you mean, relieved of my duties? I was sent here by my boss, who said I was to get all the information I could from this person so we don't mess things up." Ed told him he was close to doing just that. "No, I'm not. I'm asking her if she was really being told what to do by the Lord and Savior."

"No, you're not. You're leading her. And you're making assumptions that you have no information about. Why is it that you *know* she killed those people? Did you see her do it? Did you witness the crimes?" The cop said that he hadn't, no one had and lived until yesterday. "There you have it. You're assuming information that you don't actually have. As a representative of the mayor, I'm relieving you of your duty here."

Before he could comment, because there was no doubt to Harlan that he would, Harlan stood up and helped the cop to the door. When he reached for his weapon, Harlan drew his first and put it to the man's forehead. It was the first time in ten years that he'd had to draw it, and it made him just a little nervous.

"You do that and we'll end this right now." Harlan let his gun bite deeply into the other officer's head before he spoke again. "I'm not going to stand down and let you make this a mistrial. And that is exactly what you're doing."

"I'm not going to stand for this either. My boss is going

to hear about what happened here today." Harlan told him good, to go ahead. And that confused the man. "You're going to be in so much trouble when I get done telling my boss."

"So you said. Twice now. But I don't care. Why don't you go ahead and bring him back here with you and we'll talk about this? But not before I talk to this woman." He pushed him, just enough that he was out of the room, before closing the door in his face. Harlan turned to Ed to ask him to begin recording this conversation.

Harlan looked into the camera that was being held by another cop who was there, and stated the date and time. Then he asked Alex to state her name, which she did, even going so far as to say her name was Saint Alexandra Grace, right hand to the Lord.

"Miss Grace, I'd like to talk to you about your relationship with your Lord." Her face brightened in that moment. She looked excited instead of upset. And just like that, Harlan knew two things. Alex believed that she was speaking with the Lord, and that she was as nutty as a fruit cake at Christmas.

"Oh sure. He's the one that told me it was time for me to take out the whores of the world. I was working on that when I got hurt. I don't know why that man tried to hurt me...I only shot him at my Lord's command. But I'll take care of him for the Lord when you've released me. When I spoke to my Lord, he said that it was my duty to make sure that they didn't teach our children their ways." He asked her when the Lord had come to her about this, shocked that she'd just admitted to trying to murder the off-duty cop. "Just after we were allowed to go into our rooms to ready them for the first day of classes. I guess about a couple of months now. It's always very hectic then. Some of the teachers go overboard, but they're young yet and haven't figured it out. The parents don't care what the room looks like so long as the kids are gone all day. I had gone to my home that night after seeing what a mess I had, and he spoke to me then."

"After or before Mr. Winter was killed?" She asked him who that was. "The man that we found in your home. He'd had his neck broken, and then he'd been cut up and put in a trash bin by your home. You don't remember him? We found evidence that you'd had sex with him just before he was killed."

"Oh, Carl. Yes, it was just after that. I'd just had the best climax with him when he just dropped over me. I didn't know what was going on, and had gotten out of the bed when he just stood up with his head all twisted up. My Lord said he had used me to end his life. He was a sinner, you see. But he needed to talk to me about doing his work, and he thought that having a body to do it with would be easier on me. Plus, Carl was a sinner like those teachers are."

"But you slept with him. What does that make you?" He watched her face…the confusion was there. He decided to try a different approach when she didn't seem to have an answer for him. "What does your Lord think of you having premarital sex with a man who was married to someone else? And why didn't your Lord just kill Mr. Winter on his own? That would have saved you the added murder on your sentence. Why did he have to have you do it?"

"I didn't question my Lord. I have before, but he gets so upset with me that I try very hard not to do that. Besides, what sort of person thinks that it's all right to question the divine savior?" He said that he would if he'd been asked to murder people. "I didn't murder anyone. What I did was follow the directions of my Lord. I was making the world a better place for the children. Those whores, they were teaching them bad things. I was simply the instrument that he used to make it better for everyone."

"Make it better for whom? Not the families that are left behind. Nor do I think any of the people that knew these victims of yours are very happy with your work. Did you happen to see him...your Lord, did you see him?" She said that she'd not. But then neither had he. "True, but I'm not going around killing innocent people either. What about the bomb in the school? Do you know anything about that?"

"Yes. It was the first time that I failed my Lord. I was told to see how to make it, and that I was to set it up on a desk for someone to find and open. He was not at all happy with me. He said that I was to get her to open it on the first day of classes. But she didn't do that. Someone else did." He asked her if she'd meant the first day of school. "Yes. That way I would have been able to get all of them at one time for him. I would have too, had she done as I wanted her to. Now I have to find them all and end their sinning. Taking them from this earth so that our children will be safe is how I have to make it right. They're whores, and I needed to do as I was told."

"So you keep saying. You do realize that the children would have been in the school had the bomb gone off, don't you? All those children that you're trying to protect from whores, wouldn't they have been killed too? What did your Lord think of the loss of life of the children?" She let him know what she had been told. "So the children, they were expendable in this plan of yours. That doesn't sound like the Lord that I know. He's a forgiving and compassionate man. This sounds to me like it's the work of a woman scorned."

"I don't know what you mean. But I did what I was told, without question. I'm sure that anyone would have done the same thing, without question as I have done." He wasn't having any luck at tripping her up. She smiled at him when he sat back in his chair. "I have so much more to do for my Lord. I'd very much like to be let go from these chains so that I might do it. I don't suppose you know where that man that I didn't remove from this world is right now, do you? I have been told that he must be taken out for not paying us the respect that we deserve."

She held out her hands like she fully expected him to just say okay and release her. Instead of getting into any kind of debate with her about why she was locked up and not going to be released, ever, he pulled out the pictures that he'd been carrying around since he'd gotten in on this case. He laid them out in front of her.

They were pictures of the men that had been there cleaning the building. Men with children on their laps and in their arms. Smiling to the person who had taken the photo. Happy men, who had simply gone to work one night and lost their lives in the most senseless way possible.

"What about Mr. Hardgrave? Or Mr. Fleming? What about their deaths?" She asked him who they were. "Well, they weren't whores, that's for sure. They were a part of the cleaning crew that was in the building that you blew up with your bomb. Their families are struggling to figure out why you murdered them for no reason."

"I told you, I didn't murder anyone. I was doing the Lord's work." He could hear her temper then; it was the first time since they'd started questioning her over three hours ago. "I was told to put it on her desk so that she'd open it and all of the whores would be gone from this earth."

"You said that the Lord told you to put it on Tisha's desk, correct?" Alex looked away, then back at him with confusion again. "So he didn't tell you to put it on her desk. Why did you? You picked her for a reason. Did she slight you for some reason? Was she your target all along? What did she do to you that had you putting the bomb on her desk?"

"She was a whore, that's what I was told. And as for putting the box on her desk, yes, he did tell me to do that. He told me to make the bombs and put them around the building. Besides, it's not like she would have noticed an extra box. She got stuff all the time that she bought and made us all look bad." Harlan waited while she tried to gather her anger around her. "She was the perfect whore to do it to. Her getting things delivered to the school meant that she'd be the one that would open it without question."

"But she didn't, did she? You put it on her desk the night before, and she didn't open it when she was there. You didn't know that did you, Alex? That Tisha would be there before the teachers were to arrive? Before the children were dropped off and let into the building. You knew that she'd be there in the morning, and you were hoping for a full house when it went off." Her face reddened, her lips became a tight white line. Anger seemed to come off her in waves; her entire demeanor was hard, pissed off. "She didn't open it that night or the next morning like you had planned, did she? Instead she left it there and asked her dad and others about it. That was how we figured out that she had nothing to do with it, her checking around to make sure that she'd not been sent the wrong box. Her dad, as well as the company that she orders things from, confirmed for us that she wasn't the murderer, you were. You set her up to be killed with several hundred others, children included. Didn't you, Alex? You failed to kill anyone you wanted dead then, so you went out and killed them on your own."

"She should have just opened the fucking thing. Her

name was on it. Why did someone else get it in their fucking head to open something that didn't belong to them? Those fuckers needed to die too. They deserved it for fucking up the plan I worked so hard on." Ed moved back, the camera in the cop's hand not shaking either when he too backed away. Harlan felt his hands sweat in his excitement. He was close now to finding out the real reason for all of this, and he was sure that Ed knew it as well. "I was told to make the bomb so that I could take out all the...so that the Lord could take out the whores of the school. Because of some idiot that couldn't read, I failed. What was I supposed to do but go after them on my own? At the direction of my Lord."

"You said you could take them out. Not the Lord, but you could. What did Tisha do to you that upset you enough to want to kill her?" He didn't think she was going to answer, so he laid the other pictures of the men on her table. The one that the medical examiner had taken when he figured out which parts of the men went with what pieces. "Those men, they worked hard, loved their families and children, and you killed them. Murdered them for your own personal gain."

"No. No. No. I told you. I did not murder anyone. They weren't supposed to touch the box. I put her name on it so she'd open it." Harlan stood up and handed her the pictures of the school. Of the bodies of another man that they'd yet to identify hanging from a tree. The twisted sled that haunted him so much was there near the crater where the school had been. When she turned and looked at him instead of the pictures, he smiled at her. "You should know that you're making my Lord very upset right now. He doesn't like to be questioned."

"Upset enough to have you try and murder me? I don't think you're going to be able to do that, Alex. I've already had them remove your weapons of choice. And I'm pretty sure that as locked up as you are right now, you couldn't even get close enough to hurt me. And you want to, don't you? Not his Lordship, or whoever you're using as your scapegoat. But you…you want to get up and bash my head in." She told him she had work to do and would be free soon enough, and he'd have to wait and see. "No, I don't think so. We have you for the murder of fourteen people. I don't think you're going anywhere anytime too soon."

"I'd like for you to leave now. You've upset me, and when my Lord finds out, he'll have to take action against you. I'm his servant and he cares for me. I would very much like it if you left now. I'm busy." Harlan asked her why. "I need to pray about your soul. You're a bad man, and I think it would do me good to pray for you."

"All right, but know this, Alex. We're going to finish this, you and I. And when you're on trial for the murders of all those people, I'm going to be right there telling them what a sick fuck you are." Ed cleared his throat then, reminding him, he was sure, that things were being recorded. "You pray for me if you wish, Alex, but I'd be more worried about your own soul than mine. You think on that."

~~~

When the men left her, Alex thought about what the nasty man had said. The man was just too arrogant if he thought that he didn't need her to pray for him. He was going to have to be taken out of this world, her world, for just being too stupid to believe that her and the Lord weren't working together to save the innocent.

You have done well, my child. But getting brought here has made it difficult for you to finish what you have begun. I don't think that officer is going to let you go soon enough for you to work with me. She said that she'd be out of here soon enough. *I need for you to finish the jobs I have put you to, Alex. There is much work yet to be done. You should not have allowed yourself to be caught.*

"I asked him to release me and he didn't." The man had ignored her completely when she'd asked him. "I think he's a bad man, my Lord. A terrible man that should have been on my list from you as well. There are so many people conspiring against us. Whatever shall we do?"

You are correct in that, yes. But you have failed me again, Alex, my child. Whatever shall I do with you? Alex lay back on the bed and felt tears fall. *You have done so well until now. I will have to find another to finish this for me.*

"No, please don't. I'll take care of it." She looked over at the camera on the wall and thought about the other man filming her too. "They're going to twist up my words and make me look bad. I don't know what to do about that. They must be taken care of, my Lord. You'll help me, won't you? You'll make it so that I can be free?"

I will not be able to help you with this, my child. You will have to do this on your own. But alas, I think even you, a good soldier, will not be able to overcome this task. She asked him why he couldn't just take the body of someone and have her freed. *It takes a lot of energy to do that.*

That sounded lame even to her. "But I thought you were all powerful. That you could make things happen." He didn't say anything. "You did it once. Can't you just get someone to come in here and let me go? I have things I need to get finished for you. You said yourself that I have done a good job."

You have. Until now. His voice sounded mean, and she felt her own temper start to rise up. *I think it is time that we no longer depend on each other to get things done. You have failed me.*

"I didn't fail you. You failed me." She looked around the room when she thought she heard someone speaking. "You're trying to make me look bad now, aren't you? After all that I've done for you."

You have done nothing for me. This was for yourself. His voice sounded different, like he was...her father? *You never do anything right, Alexandra. Not even when you were little. I tried and tried to teach you things, but you had things in your head that were not right.*

"Daddy?" The voice said nothing. "You can't be here. You're dead. I know you are. Who is this? Where are you?"

She looked around the room, knowing that someone was lurking in the corner or behind the curtain. Trying to get herself free to check, the chains on her arm pulled hard on her. How was she supposed to do the Lord's work if they put her in chains like this? Tugging harder, she paused when her father spoke again.

Why am I dead, Alexandra? Do you remember that day? The day you killed me?" She shook her head. *You killed me with that knife, and then told the police that I tried things with you, things a man does not do to his own child. You made them think me a monster, when all the time it was you.*

"You wouldn't let me go to that party. I wanted to go and be pretty." Alex tried to get him to shut up and get away at the same time. "Go away. I don't want to talk to you anymore. I have things I must do for my Lord."

Your Lord? Christ child, you have no more business thinking the Lord is gonna help you than he will me. And I'm dead and gone. And I'm betting that you're going to be joining me soon. Won't that be a hoot? You and me in the same hell you put me in. Alex asked him why he was doing this to her. *You mean reminding you that you're not a good person like you think you are? Or that you're a murdering bitch? Tell me, Alex. Where is your dear mother? Did you kill her as well?*

"She was as bad as you were. Not letting me have what I needed. And I didn't kill her. I was asking her for the money for the dress and she fell." The dress. Her mother had been yelling at her because of money. It was always about money with her. So when she was coming down the stairs, her mother took a misstep. "I'm a good person. The Lord has chosen me to do his work."

His work? You mean murdering poor children? Or do you mean that he picked you to kill off women that had it better than you? You know why they did? Because they worked hard at it. You just sat around and complained that you didn't have this or that. The only reason you have that teaching degree is because you fucked your way through college. Her dad was screaming at her now, just like he had when she'd been younger. She didn't like it any better now than she had then. *What do you suppose they're going to say to you when they find that out? Hmm? That you're as crazy as they think you are?*

"I'm not crazy." The woman that entered the room looked shocked, but said nothing to her. "Come here and release me. By order of my Lord, I demand that you let me go so that I can get out of here. And I want you to stop letting my dead father in here. He's not nice, and he's yelling at me for no reason. He's dead, he should just get over it."

"Your dead father is yelling at you, and you somehow think I can stop that? I don't think so. I'm here to check your blood pressure. The monitors are a little off." The nurse smiled at her then. "You have the entire floor buzzing that you've been finally caught. People are wondering if the good Lord himself will come down here and smite you. Is that who you're talking to?"

"I'm talking to my dead dad. He's telling me what a horrible person I am. He even said that I'm going to be in trouble for not getting my degree by learning anything. He acts like it wasn't hard work to fuck those professors." The nurse just looked at her. "This happened before I was asked by my Lord to come and do his work, so it doesn't count. I'm a changed woman now. I have the Lord on my side."

"You cheated to become a teacher? Why? That's just not right. I had to work really hard to be what I am today. I had to go without to become a nurse, and you're saying that you find nothing wrong with cheating? That because you were doing your Lord's work, that somehow makes it okay?" The nurse didn't understand, and Alex started to explain. "I don't think I want to know anything about your life. You killed all those people, and for what reason? No. You just let me take care of you, but I don't want to know you."

No matter how hard she tried to get the woman to understand her side of things, she simply ignored her. It wasn't as if she'd not speak to her…if Alex asked, she'd tell her the progress of her health, but nothing more. People just did not understand what it was like to have been selected for such a journey, and to work with someone as wonderful as her Lord. Well, she was going to show them, all of them, what she'd been chosen to do.

After she was left alone again — even her father had left her — Alex thought of what she'd been doing for the Lord. She'd never once killed anyone, but she could see where people would think she'd done it. The Lord had told her once that she'd been only taking them from this earth so that he could have them near him. Alex had assumed that they'd go to hell, but he said that he didn't work that way.

"You don't take them to heaven, do you? I mean, you send

them to hell, right?" He said that there was no such place to him. "But the Bible, it says there is a place that—"

Who are you going to believe, my child, me or a book? She said him. Good. There will be no more talk about hell or where the people are going when you do as you're told. You must believe that I'm taking care of them once you have done as you are told. And that will be the end of this discussion.

She hadn't brought it up to him again. Alex did think about it, a great deal, but she never mentioned it or questioned him about it. But now, now that her Lord had forsaken her, she thought about it a great deal.

"There is a hell." Alex knew that there had to be. She knew there had to be someplace they went, not that she thought she'd be there with the other sinners. Not even for ending her parents' lives, or the neighbors that had butted into how she was living alone in the house. "My parents are there now. I know it. They were just terrible people."

"You think?" The woman sitting across from her scared her a little. Alex wasn't sure if she was real or not, and when the woman laughed, the hair on her neck and arms danced. "Yes, I'm very real. I've been sent here to ask you a few questions."

"If you're here to make fun of me, I'd like you to go away. I have my prayers to say, and I'd like to rest. They're going to let me go soon, and I have many jobs yet to do." The woman laughed again. "Who are you?"

"No one you know. At least, you've never heard of me. My daughter, you killed her in your spree. Anna Lynn Howard. She taught fourth-grade. It was her first year." Alex remembered her, and smiled at the things that her Lord had told her to do to the sinner. "I can see that you know her. She was my only child. We're only given a single child in our lifespan, and you took mine away from me. So as a vampire of considerable age, I am now left alone in this world."

"She was a sinner. A whore. And now you tell me she was a vampire. The Lord told me to take her out of this world." The woman said nothing. "Anna Lynn didn't have any right teaching children. None of the women there did. They were terrible people. Teaching the innocent to sin too. Her death was a necessary thing."

"Was it? I believe that she had every right to do what she wanted. And you took that away from her." The woman stood up and moved to the window. Alex thought she could see through her, and had to blink several times before she became solid again. "Anna Lynn loved children. Seeing them grow up into productive humans. Letting her mingle with humans, it was one of the hardest things I've ever done."

"I don't understand." The woman only smiled at her but didn't explain. "They were whores, the Lord told me that they were."

"Anna Lynne was no more a whore than you are a nice person. She told me about you. How you'd take lunch money from the children when they left it on their desks. The time that you had all of them put their hats and coats in a bag to be donated to the children's home, along with food you'd stolen from the school pantry. Then sent letters home to the parents saying that someone had taken their things. Some of those parents had to work very hard for those small items." Alex smiled at the memory. She'd gotten a bonus for the most donated items that year. "You're a monster."

"I am the Lord's servant." She shifted on her bed, trying to see the woman clearly. There was something off about her. Alex didn't know what it was, but she was sure that she wasn't there for some reason. "Someone is trying to make me look like I'm not right. They've put a camera in my room so that it looks like I'm talking to myself. But I can see you. You're beautiful, but evil. I can see that."

The woman turned to her, her smile showing nearly all her teeth. And Alex noticed that a few of them were very sharp looking. Just as she started to move toward her, Alex noticed something else, something that wasn't right. The woman had long nails and wings.

"What are you?" The woman laughed, causing the skin on Alex's body to tighten up and feel hot. "I wish for you to be gone. I.... My Lord and I have much to discuss."

"You're mine."

CHAPTER 12

Tisha moved through the grass and dried leaves as quietly as she could. This was the first time she'd been left alone as her cat, and she wanted to play. But Emma and Holly had told her that she'd need to practice a bit before she played in the woods with Zach. He would want to find her.

It had taken her a few minutes to figure out what they were talking about. She was still just a little uncomfortable talking about sex with these women, all of them. Susie was the most fun, Emma was serious, and then there was Mercedes. She was hilarious. But they talked about sex like she did her study plan for school. Like it was their life line. She supposed if their husbands were anything like Zach, she could understand that a little too.

But the real reason she was here, alone in the woods, was that she needed to think. She could have done it in the house, she supposed. Thinking didn't require others to be still. But she'd needed it, the stillness. The calmness of the woods, to think about Alex and her death.

Tisha didn't know why, but she didn't believe for a moment that Alex had killed herself. No one had seen her do it. The camera in her room had mysteriously gone out, and all they'd been left with was a black screen for ten minutes.

Plenty of time, she supposed, to have torn her wrists out with her teeth and bled out. But it didn't make sense. She had believed that she was doing the Lord's work, and that just didn't seem right. To kill herself and be so religious too. But then, Tisha had thought about it too when she'd first woken in the hospital after being hurt.

Tisha heard a branch break behind her and lay down. It wasn't hard to blend in this time of year. There were so many colors around that if she was still she doubted that anyone could find her. Twice today she'd come upon a stand of deer, and they'd eaten around her. She thought it was because she was cunning. But she was pretty sure it was because they were hungry.

I can smell you. You should be behind me, not in front of me. Damn it, she'd forgotten about that. Downwind. Lifting her head to see Zach coming toward her, she was surprised to see that he was about half dressed. And good Christ, he looked good enough to eat.

Shirtless, with his jeans riding low on his hips, his chest was covered in that fine down that was the same color as his cat, and he was browned by the sun. She couldn't see his face, not yet, but she knew that he'd be smiling. He was forever doing that. But the cake topper as far as she was concerned was his hat. That wonderfully sexy cowboy hat just resting on his head like he'd been born with it.

I thought you had to finish up the other fields today. He nodded and started to unbuckle his belt. *Mason said that you would be gone for hours yet, and that you'd be exhausted when you got home.*

I talked to your dad yesterday, and I have to tell you, he's a smart businessman. She wasn't sure where this was leading, but nearly swallowed her tongue when the belt landed in a heap on the ground. *I got another tractor...it was delivered just this morning. And we hired nine men to help me out in the fields. He said that I'm not invincible, and that I should have more help.*

His fingers danced over his cock that was outlined nicely in his tight pants. Tisha turned now instead of just looking over her shoulder at him, and watched as he unbuttoned each button slowly. When he spoke again, this time aloud, she had to tear her eyes from the fur that made a straight line to his cock.

"I said, I'm going to be more of a land baron now, and not a man working too hard to play. Would you like to play with me?" The images that zoomed through her head made her needy. "What would you like to do to me, Tisha? I'm about up for anything you are."

His voice…Christ, that lovely tone he had when he wanted her. Low and soft, like his words didn't just come to her, but floated on air at her. When she stood up, stretching as if she had not one care in the world, he moved to the big tree he was near and leaned back against it.

Let me see your cock. Free yourself so that I can look at how hard you are. You are too, aren't you, Zach? He popped the last button and she could see just the tip of his cock then. *All of you, Zach. I want to see your cock.*

He pulled his pants down over his hips, taking his silky boxers with them. When his cock was freed, straining from his groin, she moved closer to him and rubbed her furred head against him. He held his beautiful cock in his hands, and she was sure that as full as he looked, it had to hurt just a little.

"You have any idea how that feels? I could almost come like this, with you touching me this way. Are you going to lick me, Tisha? Wrap that hard tongue around my cock and taste me?" He held his cock out for her, his hand wrapped tightly around his thickness. Licking him from balls to tip, tasting his fingers as well, her cat purred and Tisha felt it. "Shift, Tisha. Taste me. And when you do, I'm going to come."

Even as she reclaimed her body, she took him into her mouth. His cry of pleasure made her want more, need more from him. And when he started to rock into her mouth, she felt his fingers curl into her hair and hold her to him. It was the most exciting thing that he did to her.

Cupping his balls gently in her hand, she rolled them there. Sliding her fingers down her own body, she first pinched her nipple hard enough to make her pussy wetter. Touching her fingers gently to her clit, she moaned and lifted her head from his cock. The look on his face, the painful pleasure that was there, made her hurt with need.

"I want to come all over you. Just spray my cum on your face, then fuck you hard when I finish. Christ, you're killing me right now. I want to come, but I want this to last too." Nodding, she slid her fingers into her sheath as he watched. "You are so beautiful."

While her fingers were busy at her pussy, her other hand cupped her breasts, tugging at her nipples hard. Her eyes never left his cock as he fisted himself, his hand so quick that she was sure that he was going to come soon. The precum dripped from the tip, and she leaned in to take it into her mouth. And when he cried out, the taste of his cum touched her face, burned into her skin until she felt branded by it. Tisha opened her mouth and let him fill her this way while she came with him.

Her body was knocked back. Not hard, but she really didn't have time to think of pain, if there had been any, before he was taking her pussy in his mouth. Zach ate her, biting her tender flesh as his fingers fucked her. His tongue filled her, licked her, and she loved it. Tisha came four times, quick hard releases that made her need more instead of giving her any kind of relief.

"Fuck, I need you." Nodding, she pulled him to her, his body covering hers as she took his mouth. The kiss was fiery, needy, and full of promise. When he tore his mouth from hers and took her breast instead, she felt his teeth graze her nipple before he bit her. She came again just as his cock filled her.

Tisha didn't hold back, screaming out her release over and over as each new climax took her. Jerking his neck to her mouth, Tisha bit him. Tasting his blood as it filled her mouth and then throat, she came again and again. When he pulled back, his body bowed from hers, blood dripped on her body from the wound that she'd created, the heat of it like a brand. She came twice when he told her to.

As he roared that he was coming, she saw his cat there, running over his skin like he was fucking her too. The climax that took her this time seemed to blind her for a moment…her breaths stopped and her heart did as well. It powered over her like a finger in a light socket would, she thought, then nothing.

When she woke, she realized that she'd been moved to their room in the house. The room was dark, but she knew that Zach was with her. His cock was hard at her backside and his hand was tugging at her breast. Rolling more against him, she felt his smile at her shoulder as his body rocked into her.

"I didn't think you were going to wake up." Shifting to her back, she looked up at him. "You're so beautiful. And I love you with all that I am."

"I love you too. Do you have any idea how much I need you in my life?" He nodded and kissed her. Gently, full of love. "What did I do to deserve such a wonderful person in my life and heart?"

"You were born." After kissing her again, he rolled over her. His cock was there at her pussy, and she knew that if she only moved her hips just a little, he'd be inside of her. "I want to make love to you every minute of every day."

"That would be great, but slightly impractical." He nodded. "Besides, tomorrow we get to bring our children home."

"Today." She glanced at the clock and realized he was right. "The house is ready for them, I hope, and my family is coming over tonight to welcome them. I don't know how thrilled Loren will be with them all, but I think she'll get used to them."

She was sure she would. But Tisha didn't want to talk about family and children right now. Adjusting her body slightly, she let him slide into her. He fucked her gently, his cock moving in and out of her slowly, but she wanted more. Wrapping her feet around his legs, she showed him with her body just want she wanted.

He made love to her like he had all the time in the world. No matter how much she begged, how she tried to get him to take her faster, harder, he set his own pace, his own way. And when he kissed her, it was the same way. With care and promise.

"I want to see your face when you come. I love the way that your face tightens just for a moment, then you scream out your pleasure." She moved her hips, trying for more. "No, you're not going to rush me again. I want to take you my way."

"But with my way we can have more sex. It'll be faster, yes, but we'll have lots more time." He laughed and told her no again. "I don't think I like you much right now."

His laughter made her heart sing, her body lighter. And when he took her just a little harder, his cock filling her completely, she pulled him down for a kiss. Showing him with all that she had how much she loved him.

"Come for me, love."

Her body responded quickly. She screamed out his name twice as she exploded around him. And when he took her throat savagely, she came again, the feeling of his teeth tearing into her exciting and wonderful.

~~~

Loren was very quiet on the way to the house. He was glad now that they'd gotten Palmer's limo to get the children. It gave them room and the ability to see each other without distractions.

Zach wasn't really worried that Loren wouldn't fit in, but he did want her to feel welcome. When she looked over at little Michael for the third time in as many minutes, he had to smile. The car seat was making it hard for any of them to hold him.

"When we get home, you can hold him." The flicker of pleasure was there and gone so quickly that he thought he'd been mistaken. "He's someone that we all have to get used to. I know very little about babies except for my two nieces."

"I met them." Loren looked at the baby again. "They're nice, but little. I guess he is too, but you said he was a cougar, like the other two. Their moms said I could call them aunt. I don't know why."

"Because you're their niece now." He looked at Tisha, who was quietly watching the two of them. "You have a lot of aunts and uncles now. All of them will be over for dinner tonight for a celebration."

"You mean for the kid." He told her that it was for them

both. "Yeah, right. I'm sure you have his room all nice and neat. Where will I be sleeping? In the barn?"

He didn't let her comment bother him. He knew that she didn't believe that, but was afraid to hope. Hope, he'd come to find out, had been dashed for this child too many times in her short life.

Zach had brought in a decorator, at Emma's suggestion, and had her decorate Loren's room. It had been really difficult to answer the questions she had for him. Such as, did she like a certain color? Did she like bands, flowers, or animals? What sort of television shows did she enjoy? He didn't know, didn't have the slightest clue if she'd ever seen a program on TV, or had heard any of the newest bands. So in the end, he told her what they were up against. The woman just nodded and said that she had it. And damn, she had it perfectly. He only hoped now that Loren thought so.

They pulled up in front of their home and Zach let out a slow breath. There was staff in the house now, a butler, as well as two maids and a cook full-time. Tisha's father had insisted that since they were going to be so busy, they might need the extra hands. All Zach could think about was how much it cost.

He was still trying to get used to having money. And when he and Tisha had gotten married this morning, he'd been asked to sign some bank cards, for signature purposes. He'd been both surprised and terrified to see how much money was now in their joint account. And the unlimited spending he had on a lot of major credit cards. His new wife was very rich. And she'd told him several times, so was he.

Not just rich, he supposed, but mega rich. When he'd asked her about the amount in the account, she told him that was hers that she'd inherited it from her mom and grandmothers.

There was also a great deal of land and stocks that came with her inheritance.

"You are aware that it's your money too, right?" He had nodded, then shook his head at her when she'd asked him at the wedding. "I don't understand that. You're wealthy. We're wealthy. I'm very good with money."

"Yeah, so am I when I have it." She told him he did. "You have it. I'm just.... How the fuck does one accumulate that much money in such a short time?"

"I told you, I'm good with money. I've invested well and have gotten great returns on it. But it's our money. You love me right? Trust me?" He told her of course he did. "Good, then trust me when I tell you that you do not have to worry about a single thing concerning money again. And if we wanted to, we could travel the world and live in the houses that both my father and I own, and never have to see the inside of a hotel room. You're going to love it."

All he'd been able to think of was that she could have bought and sold Mason and Jace together twice over, and never worried about not having any extra cash.

He looked over at his two children when no one made a move to get out of the car and into the house.

"You should know that we've already started the adoption paperwork to make you legally ours. We have also decided that if you'd agree, we'd like to have your name changed to Douglas." Loren didn't say anything but looked hard at him. "We've told you everything there is to know about us. You know that we're cougars. That there is more magic around us than there is most families, even shifters. I think that alone should tell you how much we want this to work."

"I don't know how to be good." It tore at his heart so badly that tears filled his eyes. "Those other homes, they told me that they'd love me. That they'd care for me too. They said I'd be safe. I wasn't any safer with them than I was on the streets. I want to believe you. I really do, Zach, but I'm so very scared."

"I understand. Completely. So are we." She asked him of what. "Being a parent. Having not just a little girl in our home, but an infant as well. There will be times when we screw up, I know that. But you will never have to doubt that we love you and want you in our hearts."

When she moved, he thought she was going to the door. To escape. But when she wrapped her arms around him, buried her face in his neck and cried, he held her to him. Zach looked at Tisha and saw that she, too, was crying. And when she joined them in the hug, Zach felt as if everything in the world could go straight to hell. He was as happy right now as he'd ever be, and he knew it.

As they made their way into the house, turning Michael over to the nurse who was going to stay with them for a little while, he thought of all the things that had happened in the last week. Not only was Child Like on its way to being complete now, but his home and business were finally running in the black. Due mostly to him taking on a second partner in the way of his father-in-law. It seemed that Randall and Landon were perfect foils for him...he was cautious, they weren't. But he was having a good time.

"Your room is on the second level. Would you like to see it?" Tisha smiled but didn't comment on the fact that they both could see Loren's excitement. When she only shrugged and told Tisha it was up to her, they made their way to the stairs. "We weren't really sure what sort of things you'd like in it. Even having a decorator, we were still unsure. But I think it turned out all right."

"Zach said I'd have a computer for school work. I don't know how to use one." Tisha told Loren that they'd set her up with someone. "That guy, Darin, he said he'd help me if you don't care. He said I could call him uncle if I wanted. I don't know if I'm ready for that either."

"You take your time in figuring things out. We have plenty of time. As for Darin, I think that's perfect. He's been trying to show Emma how to make a better spreadsheet than the one she has been working with. Darin is a good choice. He's quite skilled at computers and such." They were standing in front of her room when Loren turned to Tisha without speaking. Tisha went down on her knees in front of the little girl. "You don't have to like the room. We don't know you well enough at the moment to think you may or may not. But should you want to change anything—the bed, the paint, or even if it's the carpet in the room—you can do that. But there are rules."

"I have to share it." Tisha shook her head and pointed out there were six more bedrooms up on this level. "Then what? You get to inspect everything I have in there? I can't make it my own even though you said so?"

"You're not being very nice right now. Is it your intention to hurt me?" Loren looked at him, then back at Tisha. "I'm trying to tell you that all I need for you to do to your room is keep it reasonably neat, and if you don't want the maid to come in and clean up, then you'll have to bring your dirty clothes to the laundry room."

"I don't have nothing to wear but what I have on."

Zach told her that they'd taken care of that too. "For the most part, it's all pretty generic. As soon as you figure out what else you need, we'll go to the mall and get it. Right now you only have some jeans and t-shirts. And boots and a jacket or two. Underthings as well." Her face turned red in embarrassment, and Zach felt his own heat as well. "How about you go on in and see what you think."

As soon as she opened the door, he knew that she loved it. And he did as well. At first he'd been a little apprehensive about the wallpaper and things in the room. It was very girly with the tiny rosebuds all over, but he thought now that it suited the child.

The bedspread was white with a line of the same roses that were in the wallpaper down the middle. There were pink and red pillows piled high on the bed, as well as the small couch in the corner. The same color as the flower on the bed had been spread to the large bathroom that was hers, and to the closet to brighten things up. A white eyelet duster hung to the hardwood floor, with small rugs scattered around. The windows, two large ones on either side of the huge desk in the middle, were opened, but they'd had shades, darkening ones, put up to take out some of the heat during the summer months.

He watched Loren walk to the large closet. It was filled with things that they'd thought a little girl would need. Nothing much in the way of fun things...they didn't know how her tastes would run. But when she pulled the bright yellow shirt off with the sparkly horse on it that Susie had sent over for her, Zach smiled.

"Each of the families got you a little something. That's from my brother, Gerard, and his wife, Susie. There is a pair of cowboy boots in there from Mason and Emma, and a hat from Logan and Charlie." Loren held the shirt to her chest as she found the other items as well. "Jase and Holly got you the jacket. And Darin and Mercedes sent a couple of heavy sweaters to wear."

"This is all mine?" He nodded and moved into the room

with her and sat on the bed. "None of it is hand me down. It's all new and all mine. I've never once in my life had something that was just mine, and nobody wore it before me."

"I'm sorry for that. Like I told you, we didn't get you a lot. But in the coming weeks, days really, we'll make sure that you have plenty to wear. And it will all be yours. But as Tisha said, you must keep your room neat. And I'd prefer that you didn't eat in here. We don't want a smelly place."

"I don't know what to say." He nodded. Zach could understand that well. "You really did get me stuff. I have a room with pretty things in it. I have new clothes, with the tags still on them, that's mine, and things that I didn't have to steal or find in a trash can."

"Yes, you do. You've had a hard time of it. But don't expect this kind of windfall all the time. We can provide for you, keep you safe and warm. Well-fed too. But we'll have rules, not just with the room, but others as well. You'll have chores to do that you'll get an allowance for. And that money is yours. To save or spend, however you want."

She walked around the room then, touching things, but never letting go of the shirt. He wanted to tell her she could put it on, but Tisha just shook her head. He supposed it was a girl thing and left it alone. When Loren turned to them, he could see that she'd come to some decision. Something that had been bothering her, she was going to share.

"I'm scared. I know in my head that you've been really nice to me, but I keep thinking in my heart that you're going to take it all away from me. I don't want to, but I'm not sure what to think right now." Tisha said she could understand that too. "I've been thinking since you picked me up at that home that you'd be one of those nice people on the outside, but mean and hurtful on the inside. But you're not. You're just nice."

"We love you. I know you find that hard to believe, but we do." Loren nodded and picked up the framed picture of the family at his wedding. "That's your family now, Loren. All of them are yours to love you, and hopefully you love them."

"Mason and me, we fight, but it's fun." Zach had already figured out that she was goading him into being upset. "He's big, but gentle, like a big bear that doesn't know what to do with himself."

"That's an apt description of him." Zach laughed and stood up. "We'll leave you to it now, Loren. Like we said, you look things over, and whatever you want to change, we'll be there for you."

"It's perfect. You're both perfect. Thank you."

Closing the door behind them, he and Tisha held each other.

"You think she'll feel we're perfect when she's older?" Zach said he didn't want to think about it. "Yeah, me either. Let's go get our son from the nurse and show him his room. I'm betting he won't care if it's right or not."

Zach said nothing, but held her hand as they made their way down the hall. He had a feeling that everything was right. His home, his family, and his heart. Zach was the happiest man in the world right now.

CHAPTER 13

Fifteen years later.

"Are you all right, old man?" Landon glared at the man in front of him. "Well, I suppose you're just too ornery to be anything but all right, aren't you?"

"You get yourself away from here and leave this old man in peace for a few minutes. I got me things to say." Monroe nodded but said nothing more. When he walked away, going into the woods that were darker than the area where he was now sitting, Landon knew that he'd not go far. Like his family, he was worried for him.

"Got us a beautiful family now, my Katie dear. You missed a lot going on ahead of me like you did." He looked out over the expansive fields, the wheat and hay swaying gently in the afternoon breeze. "I miss you more and more every single day, I do."

He saw the tractor going through the next field over. There were six of them now, all running nearly year round. Landon heard the air brakes of a big rig as they were let off, and turned his head slightly to see what business was going on at the ranch. More flesh going out. Horse or steer, it was hard to guess, but it was making money, no doubt.

"You should have seen that little girl Loren last night,

love. Just as pretty as you were on your wedding day, and fit right in that dress of yours like it had been tailored to her. Calls me Grandpa, she does, and made me feel like I could have taken on the world when she had me walking her down the aisle." He thought of taking her hand in his and handing her over to her new husband. "Jack is a good man. You'd like him and that brood of his. Two of the cutest little boys you've ever seen. And you think they don't love her too? My goodness, those two would beat their daddy up if'n they thought he wasn't treating her right."

Zach and his wife, they'd done well by that child, bringing her into their lives and his. There were others too, that had been born or brought to his family by other means since his Katie had passed. Landon wanted to complain about being lonely without her, but knew it for the lie that it would have been.

"Our Emma is working again. That girl could never stay too idle. Even when they begged her, mind you, I said begged her to come on back and be the mayor, she turned them down. Now she's in Child Like darn near every day, making something or another for them kids to love her for." He thought of Mason. "Good man, him. I never in all my wildest dreams would have pegged him as the man for our Emma, but he's done right fine. Not just with her, but with the ranch too. Expanded again, he did. Making us not just cover them few states like we had started on, but even more. And the government, they come see him when they have ranching concerns, and those of beef. I surely do love that man. And them kids of his too."

Mason and Emma had four children, nearly all of them grown up now. But they were taking after their daddy and him, out there on the range like they'd been born to a saddle.

He supposed in a way they had been. Three of the prettiest little girls that were as mean as a rattlesnake if cornered, and a son that was the spitting image of his daddy.

"You seeing old Palmer and that Georgie? Nicest couple, they were. Miss them like I do my fishing. And you just knew that when Palmer passed that Georgie wouldn't be far behind him. Four hours…can you believe it? Just four hours separated them passing on. I guess they just couldn't be without each other none. I have to tell you, I worried for them boys when she went. Mason, big man that he is, sobbed like a little baby. Had to have me a minute or two myself, seeing them all gathered around them graves like they'd lost their parents. I'm supposing in a way that they did. Yes, ma'am, they sure took their deaths hard." He thought of when his Katie had passed and how much he'd wanted to join her. "Couldn't though, now could I? You made me promise I'd be around for them boys. Well, I'm nearly ninety now, love, thanks to that old vampire and his blood. I'm thinking I did what you wanted."

Jace and Holly had a passel of kids. Six boys and four girls. Not all of them blood, but he also knew that no one of them would ever think of it. The kids they'd brought into their lives had been hurting, nearly to the point of never coming back, but those two, heck fire, all them Douglases, they brought them around and showed them what love was all about.

"Gerard, he got himself some things going on, he does. He and Miss Susie have opened up four more of them ranches for kids. I'm telling you, sometimes when I think about how them kids benefit from those ponies of theirs, I just want to cry me a river. Those kids sure do enjoy themselves when they come out. Even though some of them leave here only to pass on that very next week, you can see by their faces that they loved every minute of it."

He thought of his own rides now, the ones where he had to have help getting on his own horse and then off again. But he knew, just like Mercedes' daddy had, being on a horse would cure what ails you. Never felt better than when he was on his old saddle moving around like he wasn't nearly crippled up in pain.

Landon looked out over the fields again. The semi was gone now, and in its place a tractor. He watched as the operator put large bales of Douglas hay in the barn and went on back for another. Landon wasn't surprised to see one of Logan's boys on the tractor. This was a family that sure did work together. He looked back at the marker next to his wife's.

His son. His only blood born son had been such a disappointment to them all. He knew that he was in a better place. Dirk's head hadn't been screwed on just right. But he was gone now, leaving them in peace that they'd seldom had when he'd been alive.

"Dirk, there are times when I just sit and bawl over some of the things that I could have done with you. You done went and broke this old man's heart. Not that you'd care about that, but I wanted you to know it." He had to look away, the dates on the marker not just sad for how close they were, but that every time he thought of that time, he hurt more. "When it comes down to it, son, I think we're all a bit better off that you are gone. Burns my soul to say that, but you weren't nice, not even a little bit."

He thought of the day his son had come at him with a bat, beating him nearly to death. If it hadn't been for the big vampire that now hid in the shadows, he'd not be here to hold his grandchildren, or to drop a worm or two in the water with one of them Douglas boys. Monroe sharing what he was with him that fateful day had not just saved him, but given him a little more juice in his blood to keep him living longer. But he was tired now.

"Anyhow. Darin? I'm telling you, never would have pegged him for being a teacher. He sure does love it. He's got him a good thing going on with the ranch and all. None of them boys slacked off when they got to be rich as Midas, but he wanted to give back. Now he wears himself a tie and goes to school every day to teach them kids about farming and ranching. Even them others, those brothers, they go in and help him out too. Mercedes, she's just enjoying being a vet. That girl, I'm telling you, my Katie, she can do her job better than any person I've ever seen."

There was laughter beyond the trees now. He looked up to see several children, all of them laughing and running through the woods. When he spied the two wolves, graying at their face and moving a little slowly, he smiled. Paddy and his missus were babysitting again.

"That little Bonnie sure did surprise us all. Four little pups born to her a year after marrying her mate. Had you asked me, I might have told you she wasn't nearly old enough, but she sure was. In her twenties now, can you believe it?" Paddy saw him and Landon waved. He knew they'd not come over; this was his private time with his own missus. "They call me Grandda too. Got me so many grandkids now, Katie love, it's hard to remember who is who."

But he did know them. Each and every one of them. Not just their names, but the day they were born. He might not know how old they were, but he knew when they had a special one coming up. He chuckled a little when he thought of old Monroe's last birthday.

"He wasn't pleased with me, you understand that. But

him looking like he ain't no older than you and me were when we wed, and being nearly six hundred, is just plain funny to me." He was powerful too, Monroe was. And one of the kindest sweetest men he knew, so long as you didn't piss him off. "You know, there are days when teasing him is about all the fun I have me anymore."

Which wasn't true. He laughed every day. And was loved more than he'd ever thought possible. He had a family like none other. Vampires, cougars, wolves, and a few other creatures that he might not know of. But he had them and he loved them.

"Logan and Charlie are on a tour right now. Never would have thought them the jet setting type, but they go off to these wild places and help with vineyards and grape growing too. They got them about a half dozen little ones now too. And they're thinking that they might be taking in a couple more. I'm telling you, Katie love, we sure do have the best of the best here."

He thought of the real reason he'd come out here today. Not just to update his missus on things, which he did weekly, but to talk to her seriously about something. He wanted her approval on something. Not that she'd ever tell him he was wrong...well, she might, but she'd be really happy, he thought, with what he'd done. He knew it was time, past time, to settle things up.

"Zach and Tisha have moved me in with them. Got me a full-time helper to come in and stretch these poor old muscles out and get them moving again. Spending all that time on a horse, it's not good on a man. And now I'm paying for it, I'm thinking." He was stalling, and if his Katie was here...well, he could almost hear her telling him to get to it. "I'm gonna. You just have to let me ride the fences for a bit first."

He'd been living with Zach and Tisha in their big house for nearly a month now. And he was loving every moment of it. They sure did have a houseful all the time, but he never felt like he was being shoved in a corner. Even them kids that were only passing through their home to another more permanent place, they called him Grandda and sat up on his knee when they needed him.

"Emma and I been talking about some things. I had her changing things around for me. I knew we talked about it before you passed, but things have changed a bit. Them boys, they need more than just a little bit of cash left to them. So I took matters into my own hands, and I fixed things for them."

He had to smile. Little bit of cash? Landon knew for a fact that even should he leave each of the boys a million dollars, there would still be enough left over to give each of his grandchildren and great grandchildren that much as well.

Landon had never worried about money his whole life, and now getting close to death like he was, he was concerned about it. Not so much about how much he had, but who was to get it. And he thought he'd done the right thing.

"They don't need money. Not a one of them has suffered at all like they did in the beginning. Made them better men, I believe. Showed them the real value of having more than they could spend at one time." Nodding, he wiped at the tears. "I surely do miss you, my love. You sure did hurt my heart, passing on like you did. But there aren't no more suffering in your beautiful eyes haunting me when I go to sleep. I see you as you looked that day you come down that long church aisle and took me as your husband. Best thing that ever done did happen to me."

He let the tears fall freely. Landon thought that at his age, he'd do as he darn well pleased and didn't care what anyone thought anymore. When he could see plainly again, as well as a ninety-year-old could, he looked down at the markers before him.

"There is more than enough money in the trust that I set up to run both the Child Like foundations, as well as the pony ranches that Susie has going." He thought about all the ways that he'd spread his money around. Money he'd worked a lifetime to achieve, and had come to realize meant very little when you were loved like he was. "I set some up for the kids too. College funds for them or whatever they might need it for."

He glanced at Dirk's marker and wondered if any of them would need it for bail money or the like. Landon didn't think so. The kids that were fruits of the children he'd come to love were like their parents, each and every one of them knowing the way things should be and never harming a living soul.

"I took care of Zach mostly." He loved that boy. Had from the moment that he'd seen him coming across the lawn at him that day he'd come for advice. Back then Landon had thought himself an expert on a great many things, but found out that while he was smart, he knew squat about more than he thought he knew. "He's a fine boy, better man than most I know twice his age."

Zach wasn't going to be happy with him when he found out what Landon had done. Emma knew, of course, as did Mason. The big man had told him it was the smartest thing he could have done, not telling Zach. But he was relying on Mason to explain it to him. Tell him what he'd been thinking.

It had taken him the better part of two years to complete his project concerning young Zach. But he'd been prouder than a pup at his first venture out in the yard when Child Like had earned national attention for what it was for. And the praise of a president of these United States telling the world they needed more men, men who thought with their hearts like Zach, to make this a better place for people.

"I got him a ranch in every state, my darling. One that can be, with the money I left for each of them, a grand place for families to go and stay while they're waiting on things to settle."

He didn't want to say aloud that they were for the dying children and their families, but that's what they were. And the ranches that were a part of each of them would hold some ponies or other animals for the children to get to see, touch, or ride should they need it. He'd seen firsthand what a little bit of contact with a horse could do to someone who thought they had nothing left in them.

The noise behind him had him turning. He saw the horse coming toward him and had to smile. He'd be checked on a few more times before he left his area. One or more of the Douglases would come on around, pretending to check on fences that no more needed checking on than he did.

"Brought you out some water." He took the plastic dewy bottle and held it while Zach said his piece. "I might need your help later today."

"You know as well as I that I ain't got a darn thing going on." Zach nodded, but didn't continue. "You know that I'm nearing the better side of a hundred, don't you? Better be telling me what it is before I'm lying next to these two causing trouble."

The moment the words left his mouth, he knew that he should have taken better care. Zach sat on his horse, that cowboy hat of his just resting there like it had for forty some odd years. The way it rested on the back of his head, it gave Landon a full view of the pain he'd caused the boy. But before he could tell him he was sorry, Zach spoke.

"You've been like a father to me, you know that, don't you?" Landon nodded, telling him he was sorry. "I know that your time is limited here, and I'm thinking on that more and more every single day. And to think of waking up one morning and you not here...well, it just busts up my heart terribly."

"I'm powerfully sorry I was so hurtful." Landon stood up, not without a bit of effort. He'd been sitting too long again. "Come on down off that horse and give an old man a hug."

Zach threw his leg over the pommel and slipped off the horse. As he made his way to him, Landon felt the years fade away. The young men that they'd both been seemed to come over him, and he relished, as he did every time, in the strength and happiness a set of strong arms around a person could make you feel. With another hug and a pat on the back, they both moved to the bench that had been set here for him years ago.

Both were silent as they dealt with life. Landon thought of his years left, and how this man beside him had made them better, tolerable too. He had a feeling that Zach was thinking of all the work he had to do, and whatever problem had brought him out here.

"When I was seventeen-years-old I was sitting about where we are now. Trespassing on your land, but not really caring much about you catching me. Hoping for it, really." Landon said he'd not have cared. "I knew that even then. That you were a powerful man. A man of reason and worth. I made it my life's work, as much as a kid could, to be like you. But there was something always getting in the way. Mostly the lack of money."

"You sure were scraping the bottom of the barrel when

you were younger. But like your own daddy would have done, you didn't let it make you bitter or mean." Zach thanked him for that. "Wish I could have helped you more back then. But like a lot of families, I had my own issues taking me away from things that were important."

They both looked at Dirk's headstone, saying, without words, that he'd been some of the trouble in both their lives. Only Landon's had been a little closer to home. When Zach leaned back on the bench, Landon did as well, knowing that he'd get to it sooner or later. But it didn't take him as long as he'd thought it would.

"I have it in my head that you're saying goodbye to everyone." Landon said nothing. He'd always thought the boy was smarter than he let on. "I wanted to tell you that while I don't want you to go on, I know that you're tired too. And that I can understand missing Katie."

"I do. More than I thought it possible, I miss her." He reached out and touched the rose that had been engraved on her granite stone. "I love you, Zach. More than just as a buddy that let me hang out with him. I've come to think of you as my son. All of you Douglas boys, but you most of all."

"I know that." Zach reached into his boot and pulled out a pretty red rose that he'd not seen there before. It was a little damaged, the blossom of it a little frayed. But when he laid it on his Katie's grave, Landon got so choked up that he could hardly breathe around it. He'd seen the roses on her grave every time he came out here, and now knew who was bringing them to her. "I love you, Landon. And if it's okay with you, just for the time you give me that you have left, I'd like to call you Dad."

Landon couldn't speak. Almost couldn't move, but when Zach put his hand into his, it was being given a lifeline. A gift stronger than anything he'd ever had before. As the two of them sat there, not saying a word, Landon tried to put into words what the simple gesture had done for him.

"Zach, I'd be as proud as any father could be to have you call me Dad. You've come to mean so much to me that I feel that this is as good as apple pie a la mode I done ever did have." Zach laughed, and so did Landon. "You made this old man feel like he can conquer the world and come out smelling like a fast running horse."

"Leave it to you to make this about dessert and horses." Zach hugged him once again. "I do need your help on something. It's not huge, mind you, but could cause my Loren to get her panties in a twist when she and Jack get home."

"You bought her the Burner house, didn't you, boy?" He nodded. "I heard it was on the market, and darn near bought it myself. I didn't have any idea what I was gonna do with it, but this is about perfect. Yes, sir, perfect." Landon thought of the house and the history they had with it. "You thinking she's not gonna want it?"

"No. I'm thinking she won't want to live this close to us." Landon asked him why he'd think a fool thing like that. "Because we're her parents, and she'd only be a few miles from our house. I don't want her to think we'd be butting in all the time."

"You won't." Zach told him he knew that. "You won't, and she knows it. Heck fire, boy, she nearly had to beg you to come out to the college and have a looksee. You are the most un-interfering people I know." Landon laughed. "She sure has got herself a temper on her. Just like her momma, I think."

"You know it. She can peel paint off the walls when she has a mind to it. And be as sweet as sugar on a cookie the next." Landon knew that was true as well. "But I thought that with her ready-made family and all, she'd not be happy to have all of us so close."

"Well now, here is what I'm going to tell you. And if'n you tell her I mentioned this, I'm going to deny it." He'd started to say with his dying breath, but didn't want to upset the boy again. "She's been telling me how she wished that she had herself a big house in town. Didn't know that the Burner house was up for grabs again, or like I said, I might have eased her mind and got it for her. But she loves her daddy and mom more than you know."

"We love her too. Very much." Landon knew that as well. "You don't think she'll be upset? I have a crew in there now making it up to date. Those last owners went and boarded up the elevator again, can you believe that?"

"Some people just don't know a good thing when they got it, they surely don't." After a bit, Zach said he had to get going and Landon got himself another hug out of it. As he was walking back to his horse, Zach turned back to him with his hat in his hand. A thing he'd only seen him do when he was being real serious.

"I love you, Dad. And I'm glad that you've stuck around for us. But if you could see your way clear to hanging around until Loren returns, I'm sure that she'd be happy." Landon said that he'd do what he could. "Good. That's good."

As he rode off, Landon sat back down. He was hurting pretty badly from sitting out here. And when Mason came back to help him home, he told him what Zach had said to him.

"You've done a good job with them, you know that. And him calling you Dad now is something I think has been in his heart all along. You've been his father longer than today." Landon thanked Mason. "You're very welcome. Perhaps if

I'd had a father like you, I might have been a better man."

Both of them stared at each other, and then burst out laughing. Mason was a good man, when it suited him. But he could be a real bastard when it didn't. That was why he liked the man so much.

Yes, sir, Landon thought as he was set down in his room by Mason, he had a pretty good life here. And figured that he was going to have a better afterlife. As he sat in his favorite chair by the window, he looked out over the cemetery once again.

"Soon, my love. Soon."

Paranormal Romance with a Bite!

BLOOD, BODY AND MIND:
A KATHI S. BARTON PARANORMAL ROMANCE

YOUR FREE COPY IS WAITING...

Aaron MacManus, the new master vampire of the realm just wanted to go out and meet some of his subjects and to figure out what needed to be done to set things right.

April and Demetrius Carlovetti own an air service and are the most trusted and well liked vampires in Aaron's realm. What he didn't expect when he visited them was betrayal. His own bodyguards try to murder him and blame it on the Carlovetti's.

Sara Temple was not a vampire. She pilots planes for the Carlovetti Airways. She had secretes of her own and working for this small air service is keeping her out of sight. The last thing she wanted to do was save a vampire, even an extremely good looking one.

Sara was only trying to survive but with Aaron she becomes embroiled in politics, the magic of several realms involving a queen in peril, magical beings, passion and love.

Blood, Body and Mind, the first book in the Aaron's Kiss series.

Get Your Free Book!

http://eepurl.com/brCBvP

Before You Go...

HELP AN AUTHOR

write a review

THANK YOU!

Share your voice and help guide other readers to these wonderful books. Even if it's only a line or two your reviews help readers discover the author's books so they can continue creating stories that you'll love. Login to your favorite retailer and leave a review. Thank you.

AWARD WINNING, BESTSELLING AUTHOR

Kathi Barton, winner of the Pinnacle Book Achievement award as well as a best-selling author on Amazon and All Romance books, lives in Nashport, Ohio with her husband Paul. When not creating new worlds and romance, Kathi and her husband enjoy camping and going to auctions. She can also be seen at county fairs with her husband who is an artist and potter.

Her muse, a cross between Jimmy Stewart and Hugh Jackman, brings her stories to life for her readers in a way that has them coming back time and again for more. Her favorite genre is paranormal romance with a great deal of spice. You can visit Kathi online and drop her an email if you'd like. She loves hearing from her fans. aaronskiss@gmail.com.

Follow Kathi on her blog: http://kathisbartonauthor.blogspot.com/

www.ingramcontent.com/pod-product-compliance
Lightning Source LLC
Chambersburg PA
CBHW032136170626
46808CB00006B/2252